"You Could Use Some Lessons In Dealing With The Opposite Sex, Ms. Dickens,"

he said softly.

"I came here to swim, Mr. St. James, not spar with words. This sort of conversation is not what I had in mind for my afternoon off."

"Fine," he said affably. "How about if I kiss you instead?"

"Mr. St. James," Cass said, assuming a long-suffering look, "as we used to say when we were kids, you're cruisin' for a bruisin'."

He grinned at her choice of words. "I only suggested it because you mentioned you didn't care for my conversation."

"Just forget it," she said combatively. "I'm not interested in kissing you, either."

His blue eyes gleamed at her. "Wanna bet?"

"You really think you're something, don't you, Ryan St. James? You must think you wow every woman on the face of the earth."

"No, not every woman." He smiled. "Only you."

Dear Reader,

Season's Greetings!

This holiday season is one we associate not only with the hope for peace on earth and goodwill to all, but with love and giving. Perhaps the greatest gift is the gift of love—and that's what romance is all about.

The six Silhouette Desires this month are a special present from each author, and are for you, with love from Silhouette. In every romance, the characters must not only discover their own capacity for love, but the ability to give it fully to another human being. Sometimes that involves taking great risks—but the rewards more than compensate!

I hope you enjoy Silhouette Desire's December lineup, and that you will join us this month and every month. Capture the magic of romance—the gift of love.

Best wishes from all of us at Silhouette Books.

KATHERINE GRANGER
Ruffled Feathers

Silhouette Desire
Published by Silhouette Books New York
America's Publisher of Contemporary Romance

SILHOUETTE BOOKS
300 East 42nd St., New York, N.Y. 10017

Copyright © 1987 by Mary Fanning Sederquest

ISBN: 0-373-05392-4

First Silhouette Books printing December 1987
Second printing November 1987

America's Publisher of Contemporary Romance

Printed in the U.S.A.

KATHERINE GRANGER

has published nine romance novels since 1982, but *Ruffled Feathers* is her debut with the Silhouette Desire line. While she says she never knows where her ideas come from, she thinks her long love affair with junk food and fast food restaurants may have inspired her to write *Ruffled Feathers*.

Ms. Granger had never read a romance until 1975, when a friend dumped a grocery bag filled with them in her living room and suggested she might enjoy them. Hooked by the very first one, Ms. Granger became a closet romance writer three years later. When she isn't writing, she teaches creative writing and composition at a community college, and freshman composition at her alma mater.

Katherine lives in Connecticut with her cat, Barnaby. She enjoys movies, theater, golf, the Boston Red Sox, weekends at New England country inns and visits to Cape Cod.

For Susan R. Derrick
From South Windsor to Albuquerque
(with special thanks to Ma Bell....)

One

Cass Dickens adjusted the neck of her chicken outfit, then slipped the headpiece on. It was stifling inside the heavy costume. But she told herself it was all for a good cause. After taking a deep breath she looked across the street at the opening of the latest Burger City. A Dixieland band was playing a rousing version of "When the Saints Go Marching In." According to the advertisements, that meant the one and only Ryan St. James himself would soon appear, to kick off the opening of the newest link in his sprawling restaurant chain.

"As if he hasn't got enough money," she muttered to herself, wiggling beneath the weight of the chicken costume. No, she ranted silently, he has to open his one thousandth restaurant right across the street from Uncle Henry's place.

She had grown to love Chick-O-Rama, the small drive-in restaurant her Uncle Henry had run in Waterbury, Con-

necticut, for thirty-five years. It was woefully outdated
when contrasted with the sleek Burger City outlet across the
street. Built of red brick, the restaurant was little more than
a box, with hand-lettered signs plastered all over the front.
There were two small windows where customers placed their
orders, a couple of picnic tables on the side under a faded
blue-and-white-striped awning, and a neon sign on the roof
that stated Chick-O-Rama—Home of the Best Fried
Chicken in Town. The only problem was, half of the sign no
longer lit up, so it really said— hick Ra —H me th Be t
Fr Chi ken in Town.

Cass sighed and turned resolute eyes to Burger City. The
combination of California redwood and shining chrome
gleamed in the noonday sun and what breeze there was rippled the multicolored banners. The governor, the mayor and
assorted other officials were on hand to cut the ribbon when
Ryan St. James showed up. A boisterous crowd milled
around, waving Burger City flags and sporting Burger City
hats. But the worst slap in the face was the bright yellow
banner that stretched across the front of the building:
Burger City, it declared in foot-high red letters, Home of the
All-New, All-Delicious Chicken Chunx.

Cass snorted in disgust. If Burger City had stuck to its
original menu of burgers, fries and shakes, she wouldn't be
sweltering under the weight of this ridiculous costume. But
no, Ryan St. James couldn't leave well enough alone. He'd
single-handedly amassed a fortune by catering to America's love affair with burgers and fries. Not satisfied with that
achievement, he'd decided to enter the fried chicken business. According to Cass Dickens, that was going too far.

She glared one last time at the shining building across the
street, then turned to inspect herself in the mirror over the
wash basins. Oh, Lord, what a mess. A foot-tall chicken
head sat on her shoulders, complete with a yellow beak and

a red comb fashioned of rubber. She could barely peek out through the eyeholes hidden among the feathers.

But if that wasn't bad enough, from neck to hip, her body was encased in a swollen mass of yellow feathers, the circumference of which had to be at least ninety inches. The costumer had tried to convince her to wear feather-covered trousers and webbed feet, but that's where she'd drawn the line. This was war, after all, so in fairness she'd decided to enhance her spectacular legs with a pair of glitter-spangled nylons. A pair of four-inch heels made her legs look even more attractive.

She adjusted the bright red sash slung over her bloated chest that said Charlie, the Cheerful Chicken, and wondered yet again if she was doing the right thing. Inspecting herself now, she thought she looked like a cross between the Padres' mascot—the San Diego chicken—and a Playboy bunny.

Shrugging, Cass turned on the rented loudspeaker system, and put on a recording of a Sousa march. She winced when she heard the horns boom across the loudspeakers that faced Burger City, then shrugged. It was now or never.

She pulled on her chicken-web gloves and picked up the placard she'd lettered the night before. Taking a deep breath, she looked toward her uncle. Along with one teenage assistant, he stood behind the counter, a crisp white apron fastened around his considerable middle, his thinning gray hair combed across his balding head, and a bemused look on his face.

"Wish me luck, Uncle Henry."

He shook his head, his kindly blue eyes filled with doubt. "You're crazy, Cass. This'll never work. That's a giant corporation we're going up against."

"It *has* to work, Uncle Henry," Cass insisted, then gave a feathery thumbs-up sign, and stepped outside.

The heat and the Sousa march hit her simultaneously. She didn't know which was worse, then decided it didn't matter. She was committed to fight to the end for Chick-O-Rama's survival and that meant even putting up with heat stroke and the threat of going deaf to compete with Burger City and Ryan St. James. She raised the placard and marched resolutely forward, waving at the crowd across the street.

Gales of laughter and applause greeted her appearance. The Dixieland band faltered, then played on, but already the crowd that had gathered in front of Burger City was drifting toward her. Cass took a delighted breath and waved the placard high above her head.

Come On Over to Chick-O-Rama, the placard beckoned, We'll Give You More than a Few Chunx!

"Hey, Charlie," a teenager shouted. "Where'd you get those legs?"

A little child tugged at his mother's hand. "Mama, it's a giant chicken! Let's go meet him!"

Cass gritted her teeth beneath the mask and continued waving. The cop who was directing traffic raised his eyebrows, shrugged, blew his whistle and held up a white-gloved hand. Traffic came to a halt as a wave of people crossed the road from Burger City toward Chick-O-Rama. Delighted, Cass shook hands, patted kids and babies on the head, then started marching toward Chick-O-Rama, her placard bouncing up and down in the air to the beat of the Sousa march.

Laughter and shouts filled the air and suddenly there was a line at the window of Chick-O-Rama and the delicious aroma of Uncle Henry's fried chicken was wafting through the air. Those people Cass's outlandish costume hadn't convinced were now drawn by the smell of the fried chicken. Soon all was bedlam as crowds of disgruntled and hungry people left Burger City and wandered across the street to Chick-O-Rama.

Cass stood back and inspected the lines with satisfaction. Once they got a taste of Uncle Henry's time-honored recipe, they'd forget all about those silly Chicken Chunx. At least for now she'd succeeded. Taking a deep breath, Cass reached up to wipe her sweaty brow, forgetting that her forehead was encased in a ridiculous chicken head. She was getting hotter and hotter and the world seemed to sway, then suddenly right itself. That was all she needed, she thought with disgust—fainting on the day when Uncle Henry needed her the most.

But there was no use in worrying about the heat now. She was succeeding beyond her wildest dreams. Resolutely, she raised the placard and strutted toward the street, dreaming of swimming pools and air-conditioning, of ice-cream cones and tall, frosted glasses of iced tea....

Ryan St. James glanced irritably at the slim, elegant gold watch that circled his wrist. He was already half an hour late. He leaned forward and slid open the glass window that divided the back of the limousine from the front.

"Are we almost there, Dan?"

The driver looked back, a grin slanting his mouth. "Yeah, Ryan. It's just up ahead. There seems to be a big crowd already. Looks like another Burger City is off to a great start."

Ryan grunted and slid the window shut. Inside the sleek, silver limousine all was cool and dark. Air-conditioning whispered quietly and tinted windows held out the glare of the hot July sun. It was a far cry, he thought wryly, from the aged Chevrolet pickup that had been his first set of wheels. He'd come a long way from that hick Texas town where he'd begun working as a teenager at the local burger joint—a long way.

He began to gather up the papers strewn over the seat. He needed a vacation. After participating in this silly formal opening of yet another Burger City restaurant, he was going to take off for parts unknown. Maybe he'd cruise the Mediterranean, or fly down to the Caribbean and—

His thoughts came to an abrupt halt. Up ahead, the road was filled with people. Ordinarily, he'd think that was a good omen, except these people were all heading in the opposite direction from Burger City. He sat up and peered out the window, not trying to hide his scowl.

He slid open the window to the front of the limousine. "What's going on, Dan?"

"Damned if I know. Everyone's making a beeline for that old place across the street." The driver squinted and peered at the neon sign, then shook his head. "Chick-O-Rama."

"They probably got tired of waiting," Ryan St. James said grimly, sitting back. Well, he'd have been here on time if there hadn't been an accident that held up traffic for miles in both directions. Then he sat up again. Up ahead, on the left side of the road, was a giant chicken, waving some kind of silly sign. He was about to sit back when the crowd parted and he got a look at the chicken's legs.

He whistled slowly—the long, low, wolf whistle he'd learned as a kid and hadn't used in years. Now it seemed entirely appropriate. "My word," he drawled, falling back into a central Texas cadence. "Just look at those legs, Dan."

"Mmm-*hmm*," the driver said. "I'd sure like to see the rest of her."

"So would I," Ryan said, sitting back slowly. The corners of his mouth lifted in a grin when he read the message on the placard she was holding. "Well, I'll be damned," he mused to himself, his grin widening. "Whoever thought up that idea had guts and moxie to spare."

"Looks like you're not liked in this neighborhood, Ryan," Dan said, turning around to grin at his employer from the front seat.

Ryan St. James nodded, his deep blue eyes shimmering with amusement. For too long, things had been easy. He needed a challenge, and hadn't had a good one in years. He rather liked the idea of the local greasy spoon doing battle with the sophisticated outsider, Burger City. It was the kind of thing he'd done once, a long time ago.

The amusement drained from his face and his eyes grew distant as he remembered his youth—the poverty and pain, the persistent bad luck, the hunger that had filled him, hunger not only for food but also for acceptance.

He turned his head and stared out the window. They were almost there now. Just up ahead, the chicken was waving the sign in the air, but she didn't look as enthusiastic now. Indeed, she looked like one hot, exhausted and bedraggled chicken. Hardly an appetizing sight. Except for those legs, of course.

Cass blinked behind the chicken mask. Everything was wavy and dim, as if the heat that eddied up from the pavement had enveloped her completely. The crowd of yelling, laughing people, walking around holding paper plates of fried chicken, good-naturedly pumping her free hand and thumping her on the back, didn't exist any longer. The Sousa march had faded into the background. The Dixieland band at Burger City still played on, she supposed, but she didn't hear it. All that existed was the reality of this oven she was baking in. How appropriate, she thought woozily to herself, Charlie the Cheerful Chicken was about to be fried.

Suddenly, the crowd roared behind her and then she was being shunted aside as the horde pressed toward an approaching limousine. Cass blinked again. Someone was

looking at her out the window, but she couldn't make out a
face—the window was tinted, so dark that features were in-
discernible.

Cass licked her dry, cracked lips and heaved a tired
breath. If only Ryan St. James had decided to open his
thousandth Burger City in the winter. She'd have made it
then. But now, on the hottest day of the year, she realized
the end was in sight. The heat and lack of air were a powerful combination.

Cass sighed as heavenly blackness descended. "What a
lousy way to go," she thought, then she fainted and hit the
ground.

Ryan was out of the car in a flash. The chicken had gone
down like a heavyweight taking the final count, the heat
having obviously been too much for it. At least that's what
he hoped had happened. He bent over the still form while
his driver held back the crowd. Ryan looked up at the traffic
cop who loomed over him.

"It looks like heat exhaustion," Ryan said, removing the
head covering. A glorious river of gleaming blue-black hair
streamed out of the mask. Ryan stared down at the face he'd
just uncovered. She was as beautiful as her legs had promised. Her lips were sweetly curved, as if she'd been smiling
when she fainted. Her long dark lashes rested peacefully
against her creamy skin and her dark brows arched over her
eyelids. Her dark hair winged back from a high, noble
forehead. But patches of red glowed on her cheeks and
beads of perspiration shone on her forehead and shimmered along her hairline. Ryan placed his hand on her
forehead. As he'd suspected, she was burning up.

He lifted her easily. Despite the bulk of the chicken costume, she couldn't weigh more than a hundred and ten.
"Let's get her in my car." He carried her to the car and
propped her up on the plush seat and began to undo the

Velcro fastenings that ran down the back of the costume. When he stripped the costume off her shoulders, he was alternately relieved and disappointed to see that she wore a leotard beneath it. He was too much of a gentleman to undress a woman in public like this, but not quite enough of one to avoid a slight sense of chagrin regarding this particular woman.

"Dan, pull in the parking lot of Burger City, will you?"

The traffic cop held up a white-gloved hand as Dan maneuvered the limousine through the crowded parking lot of Burger City into the spot reserved for Ryan St. James.

Ryan took out his immaculate white handkerchief and dipped it in water from the wet bar. Gently, he pressed the handkerchief to her brow. She moaned softly and her lashes fluttered. He held the wet handkerchief to her lips and watched with satisfaction as her lashes slowly lifted.

If she'd died, at least she'd gone to heaven, Cass reflected as she began to regain consciousness. Heaven, she noticed with great satisfaction, was cool. There was no humidity and the light was dim and easy on the eyes. She slowly lifted long lashes and wondered if this beautiful man could possibly be an angel.

Whatever he was, he was cradling her in his arms and looking down at her with the bluest eyes she'd ever seen. But it wasn't just his eyes that were spectacular, it was all of him—at least all she could see. He had dark eyebrows that were cocked inquiringly, black hair that was a little too long, a square chin, chiseled lips, a straight nose, and broad shoulders under an expensive gray silk suit. She let her lashes drift down over her eyes and lay her head on his shoulder, noting contentedly that the muscles were as solid as they'd appeared.

"Hey," he coaxed in a low, concerned voice. "You awake yet?"

She shook her head, smiling. "Uh-huh," she said hoarsely. She'd come to terms with her husky voice a long time ago, when she realized she'd probably always sound like a cross between a foghorn and a boy just entering puberty.

"You fainted," the man said softly.

"Oh," she groaned. "And here I thought I'd died and gone to heaven." She lifted her lashes and stared up at the man. Not even an angel could have a voice like that—and wasn't it illegal outside of Hollywood to be that good-looking? She dragged herself upright and pressed a shaky hand to her forehead. She had a headache slamming against her temples and her mouth was parched.

"Here," he said, holding a glass to her mouth. "Sip this."

She sipped greedily, discovering the coldest water she'd ever tasted. She would have downed it in one gulp, but he took the glass away.

"Ah-ah," he cautioned. "Not so much. Just sip it."

"Where'd you ever get water that cold?" she asked, then looked around. "And a car like this?" Her eyes came back to his and she began to suspect that something was awry. It usually was in her life. "Who are you?" she asked, eyes narrowed suspiciously.

"Your guardian angel, obviously," he said. "Stop talking so much and drink this."

She obeyed. It would be foolish not to, since her body was crying out for something cold and liquid and he held in his hand a glass of the very thing. She finished one glass of water and looked around while he poured another. Outside, the crowd that had stormed the parking lot of Chick-O-Rama was now back at Burger City, milling around the low, sleek, silver limousine parked in the spot the neatly printed sign said was reserved for none other than Ryan St. James. Just as she'd suspected—rather than being in heaven, she was in the hands of the devil himself.

She turned her head to find him watching her. "It appears you've realized who I am," he said. "But I'm afraid I'm at a disadvantage." He turned his head at an angle to read the words on the sash of her costume. "Ah yes," he said, looking up, eyes gleaming. "You're Charlie, the Cheerful Chicken." He took her hand and deposited a gallant kiss on it. "Charmed, I'm sure."

Cass pulled her hand away as if she'd been burned. "In the costume I'm Charlie," she snapped. "Outside it, I'm Cass Dickens." She nodded to the restaurant across the street. "My uncle and I run Chick-O-Rama." She paused, then added in a steel-edged voice, "I'm the competition."

Ryan looked into her eyes and quietly assessed the situation. With her tumbled mass of blue-black hair and the hectic color in her cheeks, she was the most beautiful woman he'd ever seen—and the most intriguing. He sat back and fixed her with a penetrating gaze. How was he going to handle this? He couldn't just ask her for a date. He knew she wouldn't accept. Dislike for him gleamed in those big green eyes of hers. Which, of course, made things just that much more interesting. He chuckled to himself. How he loved a challenge!

He sat facing her, his right elbow resting on the back of the seat. He rubbed his lower lip absently with his right thumb as he watched her. It was a habit he had, a gesture he unconsciously used when he was planning strategy. Suddenly, he pointed toward her outfit.

"That was a nice idea," he commented.

She appeared startled, then looked down at herself and made a wry face. "Well, it would have been if the temperature hadn't topped a hundred degrees inside it."

"Contingencies," he said. "You have to plan for every possibility when you're in business." He peered through the crowd toward the restaurant across the street. "Your uncle's, you said?"

"And mine." She sat up straighter, lifting her chin imperiously.

Ryan smiled to himself. She was proud. He liked pride in a woman; it meant she valued herself. But it wouldn't do to let her know he valued it. He'd been around too many people willing to capitalize on his likes and dislikes to share his feelings openly. He didn't think this meeting could possibly be a set-up, but he wondered how far she was willing to go to fight for what she believed in.

He reached into his jacket and brought out a thin wallet of the finest Italian leather. Flipping it open, he took out a blank check and gold pen. "Chick-O-Rama," he said coolly, "is an annoyance. A mild one, but an annoyance nonetheless." He arched a brow and looked disapprovingly out the window at it. "It's aesthetically displeasing. Ruins the neighborhood." He swiveled the top of the gold pen and the point appeared. "I'll give you anything you want for it— name your price."

Her eyes widened and the color deepened in her face. She tried to speak, but was too angry to get very far. She sat up and slammed the empty water glass down on the wet bar, then pulled her chicken costume up over her shoulders. "I wouldn't sell to you if you were the last man on earth," she declared, struggling with the costume.

Feathers quivered and fluttered and began to drift in the air between them. Ryan put a hand over his mouth to hide his grin. My God, she was priceless! The perfect target for his teasing.

"So your answer is no?" he asked.

"You betcher boots, buster," she snapped, still struggling with her costume. She had it up over her shoulders now, but was fighting with the Velcro fasteners down the back.

"Allow me," he said, placing gentle hands on her shoulders. She immediately fell quiet. She stared into his eyes, her own large, filled with fight and spirit—and something else. He tilted his head sideways and tried to figure out what that something else was, then shrugged the thought away. It would come to him. Later, when he had time, he'd remember that look and analyze it. He turned her gently and began to fasten the Velcro with careful fingers. He thought he felt her shiver under his touch, but told himself it was his imagination.

"There," he said when he had finished, "you're all set." He glanced out at the crowd. "When you're ready to sell," he said with apparent unconcern, "just contact my office." He held out a business card.

She sat unyielding, eyes blazing. She didn't take the card. "We'll never sell."

One corner of his mouth turned up in a half smile. Gently, he tucked the card between the feathers of her costume. "You'll sell," he said, completely assured.

She gave him a look that appeared calculated to kill, then opened the door and stormed from the limousine. Ryan sat back and watched her walk away, her tail feathers bouncing, those mile-long legs flashing spiritedly in the sun.

"I hope you don't sell, Cass Dickens," he mused out loud. "I hope you fight me all the way."

Two

The arrogance of the man!'' Cass fumed. "The colossal gall!'' She paced back and forth in the tiny office, staring down at the business card Ryan St. James had given her. The smell of fried chicken permeated the air.

Uncle Henry just smiled and nodded, chuckling as he counted the day's receipts. "Look at this, Cass!'' he enthused. "We made more money today than we did all last month. Your chicken costume worked.''

"Name your price, he says!'' Cass whirled, her hair swinging around her shoulders in a glistening cloud. "He had his checkbook out, Uncle Henry, and he would have just written a check!'' She closed her eyes, held a hand to her head, then shuddered. Once again she began pacing. "The insolence of the man! To think he could just buy us out!''

"You should have asked for a million bucks,'' Uncle Henry said, grinning at his niece's rampage.

Cass whirled. "Henry!" she scolded, eyes filled with disappointment. "How could you even *think* such a thing?"

"Don't call me Henry," her uncle said good-humoredly. "I'm your uncle. Show some respect for your elders."

"I'm your partner, fair and square," she pointed out. "It's about time you treated me like an equal."

He zipped up the money bag and handed it to her. "Here. This is how much you're an equal—I trust you to put the money in the bank."

Cass's face relaxed into a smile. She leaned over and deposited a gentle kiss on her uncle's forehead. "You old fraud," she said affectionately. "You're as much a chauvinist as you always were. You put up with me because I'm your brother's daughter, not because you like it."

"The bank," Henry said, patting the envelope. "Before you forget."

Cass sighed and shook her head. "You're incorrigible."

"Runs in the family," Henry said, lighting a cigar and puffing it contentedly. "Must be where you get all those crazy ideas of yours."

"The chicken costume worked, you said so yourself." Cass frowned. "The only thing is, we can't stop there. We have to move ahead, conquer new worlds. Henry—"

"*Uncle* Henry."

"Maybe get a new name—"

"A new *name*?" Henry stood up, eyes bulging. "What's wrong with Chick-O-Rama? It's a good name. It's been shining down from that neon sign for thirty-five years and it'll be good for another thirty-five."

"Henry, it's passé. It's 1950s schlock."

"Schlock! It's *my* name," Henry said, pounding his chest. "I thought it up! Me! *Uncle* Henry."

"Something like Chicken Delight," Cass said, frowning thoughtfully. "Chicken City." She shook her head. "Chicken Plenty..."

"Chick-O-Rama!" Henry yelled.

Cass shrugged her shoulders. "I'll think about it and come up with something." She kissed her uncle and patted his paunch. "Take it easy, Henry. See you tomorrow."

"*Uncle* Henry!" he yelled after her.

Cass stood outside the darkened front of Chick-O-Rama, staring across at Burger City. Even at midnight, it was alive with people. Lights glowed behind the gleaming expanse of plate-glass windows; cars drove in and out, and pulled up to the drive-in window. Music played from the outside speakers and the banners fluttered in the breeze.

The heat of the day had eased, but it was still muggy. The breeze played with her hair, which was frizzing wildly in the humidity. Cass sighed wistfully. Why couldn't she have met Ryan St. James in any other way than the way she had? Why did the most attractive man in the history of the world have to turn out to be her enemy? He might be attractive, she admitted to herself, but he was totally despicable. He toted a checkbook the way some men toted guns, using money as his weapon. Or so he thought.

Cass lifted her chin obstinately. Well, it wouldn't work with her. Ryan St. James couldn't buy her off. She and Uncle Henry would dig in their heels. They'd get Chick-O-Rama back on its feet if it was the last thing they did. Sure, in the past few years, it had fallen on hard times. Yes, it needed a new paint job, a face-lift, a new image, but the food was as good as when Henry and Carl Dickens had first opened their restaurant thirty-five years ago. Everyone in Waterbury with an eye on his pocketbook and a taste for good food knew that. It's just that the world was changing.

People didn't want to go to an old-fashioned drive-in anymore; they wanted fancy drive-in windows and gleaming chrome kitchens that produced assembly-line food packaged in Styrofoam boxes.

Sighing, Cass tugged open the door to her battered Volkswagen Beetle. The poor old thing was on its last set of tires, yet it continued to perform. It had a big heart, she acknowledged, and the will of a fighter, but she wasn't foolish enough to think it would last much longer. She put it in gear and backed out of her spot, then pulled out into the street.

A motorcycle pulled out behind her from Burger City's parking lot. When she'd driven a few blocks, Cass adjusted her rearview mirror. Whoever was on the motorcycle was following her pretty closely. He wore a black leather jacket, leather boots, jeans, and a motorcycle helmet with a black-glass cover that shielded his face.

Cass shivered involuntarily. She knew it was stereotypical thinking, but motorcyclists were often a scary bunch. Those black leather jackets and high leather boots looked totally intimidating. Then she smiled to herself. She was being foolish. Whoever was on the motorcycle was probably a real pussycat. But all the same, she wasn't going to turn on her left turn signal to show that she intended to go into the bank up ahead. No sense giving whoever it was behind her a clue to her intentions. She jammed on her brakes and turned her wheel sharply. Her heart jumped into her throat when the back end of her car scraped the curb, but she sighed in relief when the motorcyclist roared past her.

She eased the slightly coughing car to a stop in front of the night deposit window of the First Union Bank and Trust. Humming under her breath, Cass grabbed the zippered bag that contained the day's receipts and hopped out of the car. She was almost to the night deposit drop when she faltered. The sound of a downshifting motorcycle split the quiet night, then she heard the screech of tires and looked up to see the same motorcyclist who'd pulled out from Burger City bearing down on her.

He might have driven by, she realized belatedly, but he'd turned around and come back. She swallowed convulsively and clutched the bag, her heart suddenly pounding so hard it sounded like a drum in the night. There was a considerable sum of money in this bag, and she intended to get it in the bank. What she *hadn't* banked on was the possibility of being robbed.

Cass didn't even look back. Turning on her heel, she raced to the night deposit window. Luckily, Uncle Henry had filled out all the paperwork. A spotlight illuminated the surroundings, but a large lilac bush rustled eerily in the quiet night, sending shadows across the sidewalk. Suppressing a shiver, Cass reached out and pulled open the drawer. Frantically, she shoved the bag into the opening and slammed the door shut, then collapsed against the building, her heart thumping against her ribs.

The money was safely in the bank. That was all that mattered. Then her eyes widened. Who was she kidding? She still had to face some maniac dressed in black leather. An angry maniac at that, because she'd outsmarted him.

She turned slowly, ready for the worst, and watched as the motorcyclist cut the engine and reached up to remove his helmet. Before her eyes, he changed from a rabid madman to the spitting image of Ryan St. James. She simply stared, telling herself she was hallucinating. Then he dismounted, knocked the kickstand into place and walked toward her, those impossibly blue eyes flashing angrily, and she knew she wasn't seeing things.

"Haven't you ever heard of direction signals?" he asked without so much as a how-do-you-do. "Do you realize you could have gotten me killed?"

"That's your fault," she said. "You were following much too close."

"Close? There were three car lengths between us!"

"How was I to know who you were?" she demanded angrily. "All I saw was some guy in black leather. I thought you were going to rob me. Or worse."

As she watched, he looked from her to the night deposit window behind her. Slowly, his face changed and the anger was replaced by understanding. She shifted uncomfortably. She didn't like knowing that Ryan St. James could be understanding.

"I'm sorry," he said. "You're such a capable little thing, I guess I forgot that you might be frightened of strangers at night."

"How do you know I'm capable?" she countered, deciding to ignore being called little. She was as tall as most women. In fact, at five-six, she towered over many. "And I'm not just frightened of strangers," she added. "It's strangers on motorcycles in black leather that frighten me." He was smiling now. Those blue eyes were gleaming and there were laugh lines crinkling at the corners and she *wished* the man weren't so devilishly attractive!

"Perhaps capable was the wrong word," Ryan conceded. "I guess I meant brave."

"Brave?" Her mouth snapped shut on her surprise. Glaring, she pushed past him, her heels clicking determinedly on the pavement as she made her way to her car.

"Did I say something wrong?" he asked, following her.

"You're making fun of me," she said in a low voice that shook with anger.

"No, I'm not. It *was* brave of you to stand up to the new
kid on the block. Especially when the new kid is one thou-
sand times bigger than you."

She threw a disparaging look over her shoulder, got into
her car, and slammed the door. "Bullies are usually bigger," she said coolly, "but that doesn't mean you shouldn't
stand up to them." Proud of her speech, she lifted her chin
and turned the key in the ignition. It would make a great
exit, she thought exultantly, leaving him standing there in
the dust to ponder her insightful words.

Except the car refused to cooperate. The engine grum-
bled and spit and coughed, sounding like a moose in pain.
She tried the ignition again. The car coughed, wheezed, then
died completely.

Ryan rested an arm on her door and peered in at her
through the open window.

"Trouble?" he asked mildly.

Grr. "Nothing I can't handle," she said, smiling sweetly.
"I'm such a capable little thing."

"Oh ho," he said, stepping back as she stormed out of the
car. "The lady has claws."

She wouldn't even comment. She went to the back of the
car, threw the tiny hood up, and stared down at the engine.
Frowning, she poked and prodded, but everything looked
fine to her. As if it wouldn't; she knew as much about car
engines as she did about Greek.

"Have you considered calling Triple A?" Ryan asked
mildly.

She threw him a dirty look. "Not a member."

"Mmm." He rubbed his lower lip, looking properly puzzled by the engine. "Could you be out of gas?"

She snorted at him. "What do you take me for? A nincompoop?" She slammed the hood and dusted off her
hands, then spied a dark trail of oily liquid trickling from

underneath the car. Uh-oh, trouble. She bent to peer underneath the car. Sure enough, there was a gaping hole and the car's precious supply of oil was dribbling out. She'd probably caught the underside of the engine on the curb when she'd hung that wicked left to escape Ryan. But that didn't matter now—she had to think about the future. If she tried to drive without oil, the engine would be utterly ruined in a matter of a minute or two.

"Damn," she muttered, then shook off her anger. "What the heck. It won't be so bad walking home."

"How far is home?"

"A few miles," she said, then frowned. "Five or six." She hesitated, then glanced at Ryan. Did he look like a white knight who might rescue a damsel in distress? "Actually, it's ten miles," she said. "But who's counting?"

He put his arm out, offering her the crook of his elbow. "If the lady isn't too proud, she can ride home behind me on my motorcycle."

Cass considered his invitation. At this time of night, all the service stations were closed. What other recourse was there? Walk home? Hitchhike? Flag down a police car and ask for a ride? She drew herself up. She'd go with him, but she certainly wouldn't take his arm. "If it wouldn't be any bother...." she said stiffly. Honestly, eating crow was so darned difficult!

"Your car will probably be all right here overnight." He handed her the extra helmet he always carried. "But you'll need to wear this."

"But—"

"No buts." He strode to the motorcycle and swung a muscular leg over it and kicked it into life. "Coming?"

She approached the motorcycle, the helmet pressed against her middle. "Do I have to wear this thing?" she asked.

"I'm afraid so. Motorcycles can be dangerous, and besides, it's the law."

"But—"

"Ms. Dickens," he said patiently, reaching out to take the helmet from her hands. "No buts." Gently, he placed the helmet on her head, then smiled at her. "Now, hop on, hmm?"

She wished he hadn't smiled at her. Anything but that smile. It illuminated his entire face, making him totally irresistible. Cass hiked up her skirt, threw a leg over the cycle, and clambered on.

"Good," he said. "Now put your arms around me."

She swallowed, then did as he said. Muscles rippled in his back and shoulders beneath the leather jacket. His stomach was hard and firm where her hands joined. She suppressed a shiver. Why did he have to be so darned attractive?

"Where do you live?" he asked.

"In the country," she said. "Follow this street awhile and I'll tell you where to turn."

He nodded, then eased the bike toward the exit. "Hold on tight," he shouted to her, then he gunned the engine and the cycle roared away.

Her head snapped back at the unexpected propulsion of the cycle, then she rested her head awkwardly against his back. She only wished she didn't have to wear the silly helmet—it would be wonderful to feel the wind blowing in her hair. As it was, she'd have to be content with having her skirt billow behind her. Suddenly, she found herself laughing out loud.

"Like it?" he shouted back at her.

"Love it." He turned his head to the side and she saw that he was grinning. "Watch out for bugs," she shouted, laughing.

His grin widened, then he gave the engine more juice and they catapulted forward, the engine revving in the night, the noise stopping all conversation. Not that she minded, she thought as she held on to his hard body. She could stay this way for hours.

Three

——

It was cooler outside the city limits. They'd taken a series of back roads that led into the country and now Cass understood why bikers wore leather. The trees whipped past them, spectral shadows in the moonlit night, and Cass hung on, her body pressed tightly against Ryan's, hoarding the warmth he provided.

"How much farther?" he shouted back to her.

"Just up ahead."

The engine spluttered as he downshifted, then they were coasting into the driveway that led to the tiny house where she lived. It wasn't much, as houses went, but it was neat and clean and all hers. When her father had suddenly died a year ago, everything he owned had gone to her—this house, the battered Volkswagen that sat abandoned at the First Union Bank and Trust, and his partnership with Uncle Henry in Chick-O-Rama. They were her legacies, and she loved them all.

The motorcycle rolled to a stop. Its lone headlight dimly illuminated the run-down house. Cass lifted her chin, hoping he'd notice the neatly weeded flower bed, the clipped shrubs, the carefully mowed lawn. Anything she could handle herself was immaculate, but any other repairs were too expensive to tackle.

Cass scrambled from the motorcycle and tugged off the helmet. Her hair frizzed around her head in a black cloud. Her green eyes blazed as she faced Ryan. He probably didn't know places like this existed in the world. He's probably been born with the proverbial silver spoon in his patrician mouth.

"Thank you," she said stiffly. "It was kind of you to bring me home."

"Aren't you even going to invite me in for coffee?"

Startled, she searched his face. In the moonlight, it was difficult to make out his expression. She was tempted to make some sort of excuse, but then he'd think she was ashamed of her home. She shrugged. "Okay," she said. "Come on in."

He dismounted, all cool male grace, his actions slow and lazy and controlled. He looked like Brando, she thought, or a star in one of those biker movies.

She reined in her thoughts when she remembered that Ryan St. James was one of the richest men in America, and walked toward the front door. From the bushes, she heard a meow and her cat suddenly materialized, a scrawny tabby with one chewed-off ear and half a tail. She'd rescued him from behind Chick-O-Rama and doubted he'd ever get enough to eat as long as he lived.

"Hey, Puss," she murmured, bending to scratch behind his ears. "Miss me? Hmm?" The cat rubbed against her hand and began to purr loudly.

"Nice cat," Ryan said, bending to scratch the animal's head.

Cass lifted defensive eyes. Was he mocking her again? She decided to give him the benefit of the doubt. "Yes," she said coolly. "He is." She pulled open the screen door and entered the porch. Old wicker furniture sagged under faded cushions, but the plants were healthy and everything was neat and clean. She fit the key into the lock, opened the door, and turned on the light.

The living room was small and square, with worn furniture and an old black-and-white television. There were framed *Saturday Evening Post* covers grouped above the sofa, which was covered with a beautiful blue-and-white patchwork quilt that she'd made herself.

"This is the living room," she said, feeling her cheeks turn pink. Seeing it through Ryan's eyes made her uncomfortable and she walked swiftly into the kitchen and turned on the light. "And this is the kitchen."

Here, the floor was covered in faded linoleum buffed to a high sheen. The Formica table was surrounded by old chairs with chrome legs and plastic-covered seats. She couldn't do much about the furniture, but she'd stripped the old oak cabinets, which shone under a loving application of wax, and she'd stenciled the white halls near the ceiling with a cheerful colonial pineapple pattern. Bright blue-and-white-checked gingham curtains hung at the shining window over the stained white porcelain kitchen sink. No matter how much she scrubbed, she couldn't remove the yellowish marks that resulted from the iron and minerals in the hard Connecticut water.

She ran water in the percolator, filled it with aromatic coffee, set it on the stove and turned on the gas under it. Finally, she could put it off no longer. She turned and looked at Ryan.

To her surprise, he didn't even seem to be paying any attention to his surroundings. Instead, he was holding Puss, smiling as he stroked him under his chin and crooned. He raised his head and met her gaze, his face showing nothing but enjoyment. "Nice cat," he said.

She felt an absurd rush of gratitude and affection for this strange man, which she hid with brusqueness. "You said that already."

"Any law says I can't say it again?" he asked, one corner of his mouth twisted up in a smile.

She shook her head, turning quickly to hide her surprise. Her hands trembled as she took down her best cups. They'd belonged to her mother. They were blue-and-white china, so thin and delicate you could see through them when you held them up to the light. She set out a plate of homemade chocolate-chip cookies and poured the coffee and was about to carry the cups to the table when Ryan reached out and took them from her.

"Allow me," he said quietly.

She smiled stiffly and carried the cookies to the table. She was startled when he pulled out her chair. Ducking her head, she sat down, her eyes lowered to her coffee as she stirred it.

"Do you live alone?" he asked.

Her hand stilled. She raised cool green eyes. "Yes, I do."

He nodded, his eyes holding hers as he sipped his coffee. "Not too talkative, are you?" he asked when he put the cup down.

"Not very."

He nodded again, then looked around. She lowered her eyes, feeling dread wash over her. Now he'd notice everything. Now he'd see how poor she was. She raised her eyes, preparing to silence him with a bone-chilling look, but to her surprise he was unconcernedly sipping his coffee, stroking a contented Puss who was perched happily on his knee.

"Are you feeling better now?" he asked suddenly. Startled, she stared at him. What did he mean? He smiled at her confusion. "I was worried about you this afternoon," he said. "When you fainted."

"Oh..." She smiled for the first time. "I'm fine. It was just so hot in that costume."

"It really was a good idea," he said. "Was it yours?"

"All mine," she said. "Uncle Henry thought I had marbles in my head."

"You run Chick-O-Rama with your uncle?"

"Mmm-hmm. My dad left his share to me when he died last year."

"I see." He looked around again. "You're not married or anything, are you?"

"No." She lowered her eyes. That was a sore subject. A few years back, she'd thought she would marry Geoffrey Stanhope Sutton III. He'd had other plans. She lifted her eyes. "I'm not married."

"Your mother...?"

"She died when I was born. I lived here with my dad until he died last year. I'm an only child."

"I see."

She tilted her head. Yes, she supposed he did. How convenient for him that she lived alone. He probably thought he'd score with her tonight because she'd feel grateful that he'd brought her home. Weren't poor girls always grateful to rich boys when they even so much as noticed them? Geoffrey had once thought so, and she'd been foolish enough to agree.

"So we're here alone," he said slowly.

"I won't sleep with you, Mr. St. James," she said coolly. "Just get that thought right out of your mind."

"Sleep—?" He stared at her, then burst out laughing. "How do you know—"

"I know what you were thinking," she said. "I've run into the problem before."

"Problem?"

She shrugged. "It's a problem when you don't want to sleep with a man and he wants to sleep with you."

"I see. And how have you handled it in the past? Rudely? The way you did just now?"

She blushed. "It's not a question of rudeness, Mr. St. James—"

"Ryan," he interrupted. "Call me Ryan." He shifted in his chair, his leather jacket creaking. "But let's not get off the subject. I may have been thinking of sleeping with you, Ms. Dickens, but that doesn't mean I was going to make a move. You're very attractive," he grinned, and suddenly looked sheepish. "You can't blame a man for dreaming."

She looked up at him. "I suppose not, but you can make sure from the start that's all he does."

"Must be kind of like guarding a gold mine," he murmured, eyes glittering with humor. His voice feathered across her skin, sending shivers over her.

"A woman's reputation," she said coolly, "is more valuable than gold."

"Yes," he said, "but that's still no reason to think I was going to attack you."

"You asked if I live alone. I do. That's encouragement enough for some men."

He nodded, looking thoughtful. "Then I'm sorry I said you were rude. I guess you've got a reason to react the way you do."

His apology knocked the wind out of her sails. Her anger and defensiveness drained away, leaving only chagrin. "I'm sorry, too, Mr. St. James. I guess I was a little out of line."

"Please, call me Ryan." He smiled. "We're neighbors, after all."

"Neighbors?" She stared. "Oh. You mean our businesses."

"Mmm-hmm. And our homes. I don't live too far from here. I have a home in Woodbury."

A home in Woodbury, she thought wryly, was a long way from a home on the dreary outskirts of Waterbury. In Connecticut, you could almost draw a line separating the rich and the poor. On one side of the line there would be sweeping green lawns and huge mansions with swimming pools, limousines and palatial comfort, and on the other side there would be tacky little houses, battered cars and mean streets filled with neon-lighted taverns and the potential for violence. She had no doubt which side of the line she lived on. Once, she'd made the mistake of thinking she could cross it and marry a rich man. Now she knew better.

Her eyes fell to the leather jacket Ryan wore, then to his faded jeans and leather boots. They were all old, lived in, the farthest things from a wealthy man's clothing she'd ever seen. Right now, Ryan St. James looked as comfortable in her humble home as any man could. She cocked her head to the side. "Are you slumming, Mr. St. James?"

"Slumming?"

"Dressed like that. Today at the grand opening, you wore a gray silk suit. You're almost unrecognizable in a black leather jacket. Quite a switch."

"I like checking out my restaurants," he said, sipping his coffee. "I can see lots more if I surprise the staff, so I show up at unexpected times wearing clothes they won't recognize me in." He shrugged. "Anyway, I like these clothes and I enjoy motorcycles. Reminds me of my youth."

"I imagine you had a fleet of them when you were growing up," she said wryly.

He smiled slowly, then shook his head. "No, just one, and I worked damn hard to get it." He slid back his chair and stood up, Puss cradled in his arms. "But I'm overstaying my welcome. It's getting late. I have to get up early tomorrow, and I imagine you do also."

"Yes," she said shortly.

He stood staring at her, then he shook his head disbelievingly. "That was a hint, Ms. Dickens. I was hoping you'd tell me what time you were working tomorrow."

"Why, Mr. St. James? What does it matter to you?"

"I thought I'd stop in and see you, that's all."

"With a fat check?" she asked sharply. "No thanks. Don't even bother."

"With an invitation to dinner," he said, placing the sleeping cat gently on the chair. "But since you're being obstinate, I'll issue it now. Would you like to have dinner tomorrow night?"

"Dinner?" She blinked, then stared. Was he asking her out on a *date*? Excitement zinged through her, then common sense took hold. How could she have been so foolish? Of course he wasn't asking her for a date, he was going to make a business proposition to her—another offer to buy Chick-O-Rama, no doubt. She drew herself up. "I'm sorry, Mr. St. James, but I'm busy tomorrow night. And every other night for that matter."

"Now I find that hard to believe, Ms. Dickens," he said, his eyes gleaming with mockery. "Why don't you just check your calendar? I'm sure you can find *some* night free."

"For you?" she asked. "I'm afraid not. Good night, Mr. St. James, and thank you again for your help." She meant to sail past him on the way to the front door, but he reached out and caught her arm and turned her to face him.

"Ms. Dickens, what have you got against me?"

She stared up into his face, her heart thumping painfully beneath her ribs. Why did he have to be so good-looking? Why did her body have to react so drastically when she was near him? Right now, she felt slightly faint. There was a swirling sensation in her stomach and a sweet ache of awareness rising from her depths. "For starters," she said, her voice sounding entirely too breathless, "you want me to sell out to you, and I'll never do that."

"Okay," he said. "Fair enough. That's for starters. But what other reason do you have for refusing to go out with me?"

"I don't need another reason, Mr. St. James. That's plenty."

"Not for me it isn't," he murmured, drawing her closer. The pressure of his hand on her arm changed. Suddenly he wasn't just holding her, he was caressing her. He ran his hand up and down her arm in a subtly erotic way, his fingers just grazing her soft skin. "I won't be turned back by just one excuse, Cass Dickens."

She felt her body sway toward him, felt her head tip back slightly. She moistened her lips and watched his gaze drop to her mouth. She couldn't help but look at his. It was a beautiful mouth, she thought dimly—sensually sculpted and very attractively shaped. She wondered what Ryan St. James kissed like, then shook herself. That was entirely out of order. She couldn't fight the attraction she felt for the enemy if she let herself be sidetracked by him.

"Then I'll give you another reason," she said. "I'm not interested in going out with you."

"That's a lie, Cass," he murmured, drawing her head closer. "You're interested. I can see it in your eyes, feel it in the way your body is responding to mine."

"I'm not—"

He put a finger lightly against her lips. "Shh," he whispered softly. "Don't say it. Your nose will grow."

She felt herself grow weak. Why did he have to touch her? If he'd kept his distance, she could have fought him. As it was, the hand on her arm was distracting enough. The finger against her lips was too much. It traced the full curve of her lower lip, then he was cupping her face and tilting her head up to his. She could feel his breath on her lips, could feel the heat that eddied from his body. She reached out to push him away, but when she touched his chest, she went very still. Under her palm, his heart was beating as fast as hers.

"Good night, Cass," he whispered. He dropped a featherlight kiss on her lips, then backed away.

She opened her eyes and stared at him, her lips parted softly, all anger and hesitancy gone, replaced by the soft ache of desire. "Good night, Mr. St. James."

"You won't do it, will you?" he asked, smiling as he shook his head at her obstinacy. "You won't call me Ryan."

That was his tactical error, Cass thought. If he'd demanded that she call him Ryan, she would have refused forever. She drew herself up. "Good night, Ryan."

A grin lit up his entire face and she suddenly knew he hadn't made an error at all—she had, and she'd fallen right into his trap.

"Good night, Ms. Dickens. See you around." With that, he turned and walked out of the house.

She followed him to the door and watched as he mounted the bike, put on his helmet and started the engine. Its roar cut the quiet of the night. He turned in a circle, dirt and stones flying out from under the tires, and then he was gone. All that remained was the whine of the engine as he raced away from her.

She rested her forehead against the screen door. She'd been a fool. She should have said she'd go out with him. Now she'd never see him again. The ache that thought caused amazed her. She squared her shoulders and went into the house, shut the door and locked it. If that was the price she had to pay for refusing to sell out to him, then it was small indeed. But why, she wondered glumly as she got ready for bed, was that such little comfort?

Ryan stood in the middle of his sprawling living room, a glass of bourbon in his hand. He swirled the amber liquid absently, a frown on his face. He didn't notice the acres of white carpet, the long white modular couches piled high with beige and brown pillows, or the abstract paintings on the white walls. His eyes swept unseeingly past the windows and glass doors that covered one entire wall, past the huge fieldstone fireplace that took up almost another wall. He was thinking about Cass Dickens.

He saw now why she'd reacted so forcefully to his suggestion that she sell Chick-O-Rama. It was obvious she didn't have much money. He chuckled humorlessly to himself. Hell, she probably didn't have any. He frowned again and cursed his stupidity. To a woman with pride, his brazen offer to buy her out must have been like a slap in the face. Why hadn't he resisted the impulse to test her? What had it accomplished? He knew she was proud, knew she was a fighter, but he also knew she detested him.

He chuckled. Well, he didn't know that for sure. In fact, he suspected that Cass Dickens felt something else besides dislike. He recognized physical attraction when he felt it, and it wasn't only his own attraction to Cass—it was hers to him. That's what he'd seen in her eyes in the limousine this afternoon. He'd seen the fight and spirit, but what he hadn't recognized immediately was the attraction she felt for him.

He smiled to himself. He'd make sure he stopped in at Chick-O-Rama tomorrow, and somehow he'd convince her to go out with him. Hell, he didn't care about her restaurant. America was a free country. There was room enough in Waterbury for all the restaurants that could afford to stay in business.

His frown returned. That was the problem, though. Unless he missed his guess, Cass and her uncle were having a hard time keeping Chick-O-Rama afloat. The opening of a new Burger City just across the street must have seemed the last straw. He'd have to be careful how he treated Cass Dickens from now on. His crude offer to buy Chick-O-Rama this afternoon had definitely backfired but he should have known better. When was he ever going to get over this annoying need of his to test people?

Sipping his bourbon, Ryan stood in front of the glass doors leading to the deck that wrapped around three sides of his ultramodern home. Tonight, he couldn't see the view he'd paid a million dollars for, but it was out there—a wide sweep of verdant western Connecticut meadow, fringed with trees and rock walls, falling away to a silver lake where Canada geese stopped on their way south every year.

It was a supremely pleasant place, and vastly different from his Manhattan penthouse. He stayed here on weekends when he could get away, but those weekends were few and far between. He decided it might be preferable to stay here for a holiday, rather than fly to the Mediterranean or Caribbean. Anyway, the Mediterranean and Caribbean didn't have Cass Dickens, Waterbury did. Chuckling, Ryan held up his glass in a toast.

"To Cass," he said out loud, "my latest challenge."

Four

Cass wiped the perspiration from her forehead and took another batch of chicken from the deep fryer. It was unbearably hot. She didn't even want to know the exact temperature inside Chick-O-Rama's small kitchen. The disc jockey on the radio was going on about the record heat wave, but if he didn't shut up and play something soon, she'd turn him off.

"Number twenty-one," Uncle Henry called from the front where he'd just taken another order. "Two fries and a bucket, four colas."

Cass dumped four crisp chicken legs, four wings and two breasts into a cardboard bucket, scooped French fries into containers, filled four paper cups with cola and shoved them through the tiny window that opened onto the front of the shop. "Twenty-one coming up!" she called out.

A few minutes later Henry Dickens appeared in the kitchen. "It's time you took off, Cass. You been here since six. I'll take over now."

"Thanks, Henry." Cass got herself a drink, then slumped onto a stool and wiped her forehead. "God, I hate this heat. I wish I lived in Alaska, or maybe the North Pole. Anywhere but here."

"You don't have to work here, you know, Cass," Henry said. "Just 'cause Carl left you his part of the business, doesn't mean you gotta work in it."

"But I *want* to work in it, Henry!" Cass protested. "I wasn't doing anything particularly thrilling with my life managing the produce department at the supermarket, you know."

"You could go back to Yale and finish working on your degree," Henry suggested.

"No!" Cass said sharply. "I'm never going back there."

"Cassie," her uncle said gently. "Why not? You had a full scholarship and you just threw it away. Geoff Sutton isn't there anymore, he's graduated. Why not go back and do something with your life?"

"What's Geoff got to do with anything?" Cass demanded. "Dropping out of Yale didn't have anything to do with Geoffrey Sutton, I'll have you know."

"Cass," Henry said, shaking his head sadly, "come on, this is your uncle you're talking to. You think I don't know about what happened with you two?"

Cass kept her eyes down, then finally lifted them to her uncle. "I suppose Dad told you everything," she said morosely.

"He didn't say a word. I just knew. Heck, how could I not know—you two comin' in here every night that summer, making eyes at each other—then all of a sudden you breakin' up just before Christmas?"

Cass sipped her cola, remembering her failed relationship with Geoffrey Sutton. She'd met him at Yale during her junior year of a full four-year scholarship. Geoffrey was a senior—older, sophisticated, good-looking—the kind of boy she'd always dreamed about. They'd dated all year, and that summer their relationship had deepened. She knew she was in love with him and he told her he loved her. Just before Christmas of her senior year, he'd invited her home with him and she'd thought he was going to ask her to marry him. Instead, she'd found out his engagement was just about to be announced. Cass wasn't right for him it seemed. He needed a wife who came from a similar background, who would fit in with his high-powered and wealthy lifestyle.

She broke off her train of thought. It never did any good to dredge up old memories. They were better off buried. At least they didn't hurt anyone that way. "All right, so I did drop out because of what happened between Geoff and me, but now I know I never really belonged there anyway."

"Poppycock!" her uncle said, putting another batch of chicken in the fryer. "You've got as much right to be at Yale as anyone. It's a sin to waste the brain God's given you, Cassie."

"Who's wasting it?" she said, jumping off the stool and kissing her uncle on his bald spot. "Single-handedly—because I can't count on you, you old goat—I'm going to save Chick-O-Rama from extinction."

"Let me alone, will ya?" he groused, waving her away irritably as he rubbed his bald spot. "Cassie, I *hate* it when you do that!"

"That's because you can't face reality, Henry," Cass said affably. "You pretend you don't have a bald spot just like you pretend there aren't any problems with Chick-O-Rama."

"Don't call me *Henry*," he shouted, his face getting red.

"Why not?" Cass asked cheerfully. "That's your name, isn't it? What else should I call you?"

"*Uncle* Henry!" he shouted in response. "Uncle! Uncle! Uncle!"

Cass put a hand to her ear. "Did I hear someone crying uncle?" Laughing, she ducked when he threw a damp rag at her, then took off her apron, scooped up her pocketbook and sailed out the door. She had the rest of the day free and she was going to cool off. The public swimming pool would be filled with kids, but it would just have to do. She wore a bikini under her T-shirt and jeans, and she had every intention of putting it to good use.

But she hadn't reckoned on Ryan St. James. When she walked out of Chick-O-Rama, she came to a sudden halt. He was leaning against her VW, his arms folded across his chest. He wore faded jeans and a blue-and-white-striped shirt. It was an oversize, updated version of the classic button-down shirt. Its long sleeves were rolled up to the elbows and it was unbuttoned halfway down the front. Cass took a deep breath at the sight of the dark hair that covered his muscular chest.

"What are you doing here?" she demanded.

"Friendly, aren't you?"

"To my friends, yes," she responded coolly. "Now what do you want?"

"It's not what, it's who."

She shouldered her way past him and flung open the car door. "I suppose you want to make another offer to buy Chick-O-Rama."

"No, I just wanted to see you." He propped his chin on his arms on top of the car door and smiled at her. "I see you got your car fixed."

"Give the man an A for observation."

Her sarcasm didn't seem to faze him. "What was wrong with it?"

"Nothing serious," she said. "Just a hole in the oil line." She folded herself into the seat and yanked the door shut. Ryan stepped back and shoved his hands into his back pockets. She looked up at him, wishing his jeans weren't quite so tight, that he didn't stand wide-legged that way, looking like Springsteen, only ten times better.

"You going anywhere now?" he asked.

"No," she said, smiling sweetly. "I thought I'd just sit in the car and gaze at Chick-O-Rama all afternoon and hope I get heat stroke."

"Whew! I better watch out if I ever kiss you," he said, grinning. "That tongue of yours is sharper than a razor."

"Don't lose any sleep over it. There's not much of a chance you'll ever get within five feet of me again, much less kiss me." With that, she turned the key in the ignition. The engine coughed twice, then jerked to life. "See you around, Mr. St. James," she called and roared off.

She had gone half a block when she saw his motorcycle in the rearview mirror. Instead of being angry, she felt incredibly happy. Which was totally ridiculous, since she didn't want to see him again. Or did she?

At a red light, Ryan rode his cycle up next to her window and sat gunning his engine. "Want to stop for a bite to eat?" he yelled over the roar of his engine.

"No," she shouted.

"How about a cold drink?"

"No."

He gunned his engine again and she thought he'd given up, then he shouted, "Okay, how about a movie?"

She almost laughed. "No!"

The light changed and she hit the gas. The VW coughed, hesitated, gurgled, then chugged off. Next to her, Ryan's motorcycle kept pace, neck and neck. Angrily, she floored the accelerator and miraculously the VW pulled away from the cycle. At the next light, she stopped and Ryan pulled up right next to her again.

"Want to go bowling?" he shouted.

"Bowling?" She couldn't help it, she began to laugh.

He shrugged and grinned at her. "What else is there to do on a hot day?"

"I'm going swimming," she shouted over the roar of his engine, then took off when the light changed to green.

He followed her all the way to the town pool. She took her towel and got out of her car and locked it, ignoring him as he pulled up next to her. Fifty feet away, the public pool was filled with screaming kids. Blond, brown, and black heads bobbed up and down. Water sloshed over the sides and splashed into the air, shattering into brilliant rainbows. Boom boxes splintered the air. The lifeguard blew his whistle, then shouted at some kids.

"This is where you swim?" Ryan asked.

Cass turned cool eyes on him. "I'm afraid the minions haven't finished my indoor pool yet." She sniffed. "For now, this will have to do." She pushed open the gate in the chain-link fence and approached the pool. A few adults sat in lawn chairs on the perimeter, but none braved the crowd of kids who screamed and splashed in the pool itself.

"I didn't mean it that way," Ryan said from just behind her.

She turned and looked at him. "What way did you mean it?"

He searched her eyes. "If I tell you what I meant, you'll take it wrong, so what's the use?"

"Why don't you give it a try, Mr. St. James? It might do you good to try to communicate with the lower classes."

"You really have a chip on your shoulder, don't you?"

Her head snapped back. "No!" she said heatedly, "I—"

"Oh, yes, you do," he interrupted. "You've decided that you don't like me and you're not even going to give me a chance."

"That's not true!"

"Then come home with me," he said quietly. "I do have an indoor pool." He looked up at the sky, then back at her, his eyes taunting. "Though the day's so nice, we could always swim in the backyard pool. Or maybe we could walk down to the pond on my property."

"Don't rub it in, Mr. St. James. Your money doesn't impress me."

"Strange," he mused. "I thought it did."

She had to look away. He was far too perceptive and she wasn't very good at pretending, so she looked at the pool. In the deep end, three boys began a spirited game of Frisbee. With a lusty yell, a teenager dived feetfirst off the diving boat. Mothers yelled and babies cried. Screams and shouts and laughter punctuated the constant din. Outside the fence, two dogs barked raucously as they chased each other.

It might not be the most beautiful spot, but this was her world. She'd come here to swim every summer since she was six years old. She knew the lifeguards, the kids who cavorted in the pool, and the mothers who sat on the sidelines and watched their children with indulgent eyes. Yet it was tempting to think of swimming in a private pool, away from this noise and the heat that radiated from the asphalt-covered playground. If only Ryan wasn't Ryan St. James— the enemy.

"You can't do it, can you?" he taunted. "You can't put aside your prejudice against me, even if it means enjoying yourself."

"Prejudice!" Her green eyes flashed angrily. "It isn't prejudice, Mr. St. James!"

"Then what is it?" he asked softly. "Are you afraid of me?"

"Of course not," she scoffed.

"If it isn't prejudice or fear that keeps you from accepting my invitation, what is it?" His eyes searched hers. "Perhaps you're really afraid of yourself...."

She glared at him angrily. He was always throwing out challenges she couldn't resist. "All right," she said coolly. "I'll go with you, but only under one condition."

"Name it."

"You mustn't talk about business, not even once. If you so much as mention buying Chick-O-Rama, I'll leave, Mr. St. James, and that's a promise."

He whipped out mirrored aviator sunglasses and put them on. "Done, Ms. Dickens," he said and smiled disarmingly. "Anything else I can do for you?"

"Wipe that disgusting smirk off your face," she snapped, and whirled on her heel and stalked to her car.

She followed Ryan through Waterbury into the country. They drove for miles over winding, tree-shaded roads, then he turned into a narrow driveway that twisted through overgrown woods. As they rounded a final curve Cass coasted to a stop, staring at the house before her.

Set in a clearing surrounded by towering trees, it was a modern mixture of redwood and glass, with angled peaks that soared into the cloudless blue sky. On both sides, wooden decks extended from the house and she could see that the deck must wrap around the back. Mammoth fieldstone chimneys rose from either end of the house like protective arms raised high.

Faced with the tangible evidence of Ryan's wealth, Cass felt like putting her car in gear and driving away, but he seemed to sense her hesitation. Suddenly he was beside her, opening the car door and looking down at her.

"The pool's in the back," he said. "But I'll take you on a tour of the house, if you like."

"That won't be necessary," she said shortly, getting out and slamming the car door. "I came here to swim, not ogle your creature comforts."

"You'll need a bathing suit."

"I'm wearing one underneath my clothes," she said. "Some of us learn to make do with very little." He smiled, but his eyes remained sheltered behind the mirrored sunglasses, and all Cass saw was her own adamant stance.

"Remind me to tell you about making do sometime, Ms. Dickens," he said gently. "It might be most instructive."

"Nothing you could say to me would ever be very instructive, I'm sure, Mr. St. James," she said coolly. "Except perhaps about making money."

Slowly, he reached up and removed his sunglasses and suddenly she felt her mouth go dry. Something in his eyes warned her she'd gone too far.

"On the contrary," he said softly. "I think I could teach you quite a bit, and it wouldn't have a thing to do with finances."

She couldn't speak, could only stare up at him as if mesmerized. Her heart began to clamor in her breast, her breathing became shallow. He was devastatingly attractive and much too close. She could see the laugh lines at the corners of his eyes, the sensual curve of his lips that seemed to mock her. Slowly, she backed away, only to thump into her car.

He reached out and put a hand on the roof of the car, effectively penning her in. Her senses were assailed by his nearness. She smelled the faint, provocative odor of his after-shave, saw the dark hair on his tanned chest, heard the steady ticking of the watch on his powerful wrist.

Slowly, he reached out and fingered a lock of her hair. "You could use some lessons in dealing with the opposite sex, Ms. Dickens," he said softly. "Don't you agree?"

Somehow she found her voice. "No, Mr. St. James, I don't. Until you came along, I had no trouble at all dealing with—I mean..." She broke off, horrified to feel her face turning pink. She began again, determined to remain cool. "I came here to swim, Mr. St. James, not spar with words. This sort of conversation is not what I had in mind for my afternoon off."

"All right," he said, shrugging affably. "If you insist..."

"I do."

"Fine," he said. "How about if I kiss you instead?"

"Mr. St. James," she said, folding her arms and assuming a long-suffering look, "as we used to say when we were kids, you're cruisin' for a bruisin'."

He broke into a grin. "I only suggested it because you mentioned you didn't care for my conversation."

"Just forget it," she said, lifting her chin combatively. "I'm not interested in kissing you either."

His blue eyes gleamed at her. "Wanna bet?"

"You really think you're something, don't you, Ryan St. James? You must think you wow every woman on the face of the earth."

"No, not every woman. Only you."

She stared at him, so angry she could hardly think, much less speak. "I—" She broke off and started over: "You—" Exasperated, she pushed past him and stalked toward the house. "Just show me the pool," she commanded. "I have a burning desire to drown you in it!"

Ryan escorted her into a cavernous hallway with a flagstone floor and walls covered in golden pine, then into the living room, with its wall of windows and sliding glass doors that led to the deck.

Spread before them was a view so magnificent it took her breath away. Rolling meadows sprinkled with wildflowers stretched into the distance toward a gleaming silver lake. Low rock walls formed a boundary on both sides, as if holding back the dense forest that surrounded the sweeping meadows. A few towering maples and oaks dappled the meadow with shade, and three chestnut horses grazed placidly, their coats gleaming in the afternoon sun.

Cass stared at the scene, then swallowed uncomfortably. She didn't belong here, never would. This was part of that world she didn't understand—the world of money and social standing, of prestige, blue blood and privilege. She was reminded of Geoff Sutton's home, so different from Ryan's, yet so very similar. She'd only visited it once, but it was permanently etched in her memory, a painful reminder that she hadn't belonged.

Now she was with a man who affected her even more than Geoff had. Somehow she had to combat the attraction she felt for Ryan St. James. If she let herself fall for him it would be even more disastrous than her experience with Geoff.

She turned back to Ryan. "This is all very impressive, Mr. St. James, but I thought we came here to swim."

"The pool's right over there," he said, leading her onto the deck. He pointed to the right. "Make yourself at home. I'll just change into a suit, then I'll be right back."

Cass watched him walk away, her eyes troubled. How ironic! The one thing she would never be able to do was make herself at home here. Her experience with Geoff had showed her that; she'd never fit into a world where money mattered more than people, where love came second to lineage and bloodlines.

Five

Cass sighed contentedly. Just for this afternoon, she'd put her misgivings aside and enjoy herself. This setting was too magnificent, the day too beautiful to spoil by standing on her militant principles. She pulled her shirt over her head and dropped it on a chair, then stepped out of her jeans. Taking a rubber band from her jeans pocket, she pulled her hair back at the nape of her neck, secured it with the rubber band, then stood looking around, lost in the beauty of the place.

Surrounded by low shrubs and bushes, the pool fit into its setting as if it were a natural pond. Large wooden barrels filled with a colorful assortment of geraniums, petunias, and marigolds sat on the surrounding brick terrace. The lowest level of the three-tiered deck that wrapped around the house ended where the terrace began and both the terrace and deck were furnished with white chaise lounges and chairs.

Ryan's return interrupted her reverie. Turning, she simply stared. He wore dark swimming trunks and the same blue-and-white-striped shirt he'd worn earlier, but now it was unbuttoned all the way, exposing his powerful chest and flat stomach. She swallowed uneasily, her awareness of him making her more conscious of the skimpy bikini she wore.

"It's beautiful," she said, gesturing vaguely around them.

"Yes," he mused, his gaze drifting down her figure. "Very beautiful."

She ignored his compliment. "If I owned this place," she said, "you wouldn't be able to get me away from it. I'd run my business from right here by the pool."

"Your secretaries would like that, no doubt," he said.

"Wouldn't yours?"

"They would, but I wouldn't."

"No?"

He shook his head. "I come here to relax. If my work were here, where would I go to relax?"

"You have a point, I suppose, but I still think it's a shame to use this place only on weekends."

"Actually, I don't even get here that often. I've been tied up practically every weekend this past year. As a matter of fact, I have to leave early tomorrow morning to get back to New York."

"I see...." Cass realized she was sorry he wasn't going to be around. Which was illogical, since she kept claiming she didn't like him. By rights, she should be glad he was leaving. Or was she just telling herself that to keep from facing the fact that she was attracted to him? That thought was enough to galvanize her into action. "Enough talk, Mr. St. James, I'm going to take advantage of the opportunity to do fifty laps undisturbed."

"Fifty!"

She laughed at the expression on his face. Why did she feel as if she might actually *like* the guy if she ever got to know him? "Care to join me?"

"Not on your life. Not for fifty laps, anyway. I might manage a couple dozen."

"Why, Mr. St. James," she said, her eyes twinkling mischievously, "your age is showing."

"You've got to stop calling me by my last name, Cass. I'm off work now, not in some godforsaken board room. Please call me Ryan."

She smiled at the look of exasperation on his face. "Okay," she said, "I'll make a deal with you. When we talk business, I'll call you Mr. St. James. If you stay off the subject, I'll call you Ryan."

"Why, Cass Dickens," he said, chuckling with self-satisfaction, "I do believe you've just given me the only excuse I need to never talk business with you again."

She stared at him, feeling both pleased and worried. Could it be that Ryan St. James wanted to be with her simply because he was attracted to her? Was it possible that Chick-O-Rama wasn't even on his mind?

Of course it's possible, she thought to herself. But just remember one thing: Geoff Sutton was interested in you too, and if there's one thing you learned from Geoff, it was that rich men might sleep with poor women, but they almost never marry them.

Tossing her head in annoyance, Cass dove into the pool. She was determined not to repeat her mistakes with Ryan St. James.

Cass's lithe body sliced through the water effortlessly. As she completed lap after lap, her strokes slowed and her muscles loosened until she finally turned on her back and floated peacefully.

She could float like this forever, she thought blissfully, her eyes closed, a smile curving her lips. She was without a care in the world— Her reverie ended abruptly and she lost her balance. Before she could right herself, she bumped into Ryan.

She gasped and tried to scramble to her feet, realizing too late that she wasn't in the shallow end. Everything was blurred as water washed over her. A momentary sense of panic gripped her, then she was pulled into strong arms and held against Ryan's chest.

"I—" she spluttered.

"Are you all right?" Ryan asked when he'd brought her to the edge of the pool.

They stood waist-high in the pool with water streaming down their shoulders and arms. Cass blinked the water from her eyes and stared at him, her heart pounding, her palms flattened against his chest. She was excruciatingly aware of his body pressed against hers, of the warmth and slick wetness of his skin, the hardness of his muscles. Then her attention was captured by his eyes. She felt a strange jolt deep in her midsection, as if something inside her had short-circuited and a glowing warmth spread through her. She knew she had to act quickly or things would easily get out of control.

"I'm fine," she said, sounding entirely too breathless. "You can let go of me now."

"No," he said softly. "I'm afraid I can't."

"You can't?" She stared into his eyes, transfixed.

"Mmm-mm," he murmured, his gaze traveling lazily to her lips. "I can't. It would be an entirely stupid move on my part if I did."

"You…" She moistened her lips and started over. "I can manage now," she said. "You really can let me go."

"But I don't want to let go, Cass," he murmured, running his hands down her back. "I like holding you."

"I don't think it's a very good idea," she said breathlessly, but even as she spoke, she knew she was lying.

"No?" he murmured. The corner of his mouth lifted in lazy amusement. He drew her closer, his lips hovering over hers. "Are you sure?"

She tried to resist him, but her body responded immediately to him. Yet some part of her brain must have continued to function, or perhaps somewhere deep inside she knew that continuing to say no would draw out this wonderful game....

"Yes," she murmured. "I'm sure...."

"Why don't I believe you?" he whispered, his lips so close to hers they almost touched.

She felt her eyelids grow heavy, her breathing deepen. She slid her hands over his chest and told herself she wanted him to stop, but she knew it wasn't true. He tightened his hold and pressed his body intimately against hers.

"Tell me you don't want this," he whispered. "I dare you to say it."

"I..." She tried to speak, but the words wouldn't come.

"Say my name, Cass," he whispered.

"Ryan," she breathed, every atom of her body drawn to him.

"You smell so sweet," he said, nuzzling the soft skin just under her ear. Her lashes drifted down and somehow her hands moved up his chest and around his neck. "Do you taste as sweet, Cass?" he murmured.

When her head tipped back he brushed his lips against hers and she knew she was lost—there was no fighting him. She felt as if she were butter, melting under the heat of the sun.

He teased her, lifting his lips just out of reach. She felt a growing, almost insatiable need, a dizzying, wonderful reeling in the pit of her stomach. She slid her fingers into his hair and gazed into his eyes, her own dark with desire. *"Do I taste as sweet?"* she asked, her voice even throatier than usual.

His eyes burned into hers, then his lips touched hers once, twice, three times. "Sweeter," he murmured, nibbling a delicious line down the sweep of her neck to the pulsing hollow of her throat. "Much sweeter...."

Her breath caught and her eyes closed as he trailed kisses back up her neck to just beneath her ear. Then he gently flicked his tongue into her ear. Her senses were assaulted by the feel of his firm, muscled body, the heat radiating from his skin, the soft hair on his chest. Slowly she inhaled his musky scent, which mingled with his after-shave, and listened to the resonance of his low voice filled with dusky heat.

"Kiss me, Cass." Gently, he moved his hands over her back in intimate circles. "Open your mouth for me. Let me kiss you the way I want to."

She moaned softly and parted her lips and his tongue found hers. Attuned only to Ryan, she tumbled headfirst into a world of shining light, of strong arms and heated kisses. Nothing else existed, only him.

But when he touched her breast, she woke up. It was too soon for this to happen. She leaned back in protest and he dropped his hand to his side.

"I'm sorry, Cass," he said gently. "I had no right to touch you like that."

She searched his eyes, suddenly remembering Geoff, who'd never taken no for an answer. She'd been so besotted with him, she'd thought that meant she was irresistible. It hadn't hit her until this moment that it might have meant

Geoff wasn't sensitive to her needs. Something wasn't right. She'd spent five years hating the super-rich, when maybe the real problem was just one rich man, Geoff Sutton.

She shook off the bewildering realization. She wasn't thinking clearly now; she was still reeling from her reactions to Ryan. "It's too soon," she said. "An hour ago I was threatening to drown you and now..."

He grinned. "And now you're the one doing the drowning, right?"

His teasing was just what she needed to get her equilibrium back. "Ha!" she said, turning and wading toward the steps in the shallow end of the pool. "What a typical egotistical male response!"

The pleasant rumble of his low laughter followed her. "You just won't admit it, will you, Cass?"

"Admit what?" she asked, turning on the top step of the pool to stare down at him.

He stood waist-deep in the water, his hands on his hips, laughing up at her. "That you're crazy about me."

"Crazy?" It was her turn to laugh. "*You're* the one who's crazy, Mr. St. James!" She rolled her eyes and put her own hands on her hips. "Just because a woman gives a guy a kiss or two, he thinks she's crazy about him. If that doesn't beat all!"

"So it's back to 'Mr. St. James,' eh?" he asked, grinning up at her.

"It never stopped being Mr. St. James," she said, stepping out of the pool and walking toward her towel.

"Liar," he taunted.

His voice was much too close. She whirled around and saw him advancing slowly toward her. She went very still. Water cascaded off his hard body, leaving no doubt just how masculine he was. He looked so good she wasn't sure she could possibly resist him if he got any closer. She picked up her towel and held it in front of her, like an ineffectual shield. "I think I'd better be going, Mr. St. James."

"Ryan," he said evenly, coming to a stop in front of her. "You promised to call me Ryan. Are you the kind of woman who goes back on her promises?"

"Perhaps I should clarify that promise. When I said I'd call you Ryan if we didn't discuss business, I didn't mean to imply I wanted a more personal relationship."

"All or nothing, eh, Cass?"

"Precisely. And in your case, it's most definitely nothing."

He narrowed his eyes and cocked his head as he studied her. "Why?" he finally asked. "What have you got against me, besides the fact that I opened a business across from yours?"

Relief flooded through her. If he thought she was still thinking about business, her ruse was working. Maybe he wouldn't discover how much she was attracted to him, or why her attraction scared her silly. "Isn't that enough?" she asked coolly.

"Frankly, no. It's a free country, Cass. What's so terrible about my giving you and your uncle a little competition?"

"A little?" She laughed shortly. "You've got to be kidding! That's like saying Jonah shouldn't have been scared of the whale."

"Ah, so that's it—you're scared of me."

"No!" she said sharply. "That's not what I meant and you know it."

"Then what did you mean?"

Cass dropped her towel and began to put on her jeans. "Thanks for inviting me." She glanced at the sky, where dark clouds were piling up in the west. "It looks like it might rain soon. I better be going."

"You didn't answer my question."

She pulled her T-shirt over her head and threw him a smile as she turned to go. "No time to, I'm afraid. I really do have to be going, Mr.—" Before she could finish, she was brought up short by his hand on her arm.

"I don't think it's business that's got you worried at all, Cass Dickens," he said lazily. "I think it's something more personal."

"I..." She licked her lips. "I don't know what you mean."

"I think you do."

She shook her head, her heart thumping madly. "Really, I don't." She tried to loosen his grip on her arm, but it did no good. He moved his hand lightly up and down her arm, sending a pleasant frisson of awareness through her.

"Don't go, Cass," he said softly. "Stay and have supper with me." He smiled, and his entire face lit up. "You're looking at a first-class cook. I may have started out working on the grill in a greasy spoon in Texas, but I've gone on to bigger and better things." He dropped his hold on her arm and rubbed his hands together energetically. "Swimming worked up my appetite. What would you like? Steak? Chicken on the grill? Ribs drowning in a barbecue sauce?"

She simply stared. Had he really started out working as a short-order cook? But that didn't make sense; he was Ryan St. James, one of the richest, most successful men in the country.... She shook herself. It wouldn't do to let him sweet-talk her. "I'm sorry, Ryan, but I can't stay."

"Why?" he asked. "Have you got a date tonight?" She shook her head mutely. "Are you expecting company?" Again, she shook her head. "Then stay with me, Cass."

Her hesitation was all he needed. He took her hand and pulled her toward the house. "Come on, Cass. While I get supper ready, you can shower. That wet suit must be pretty uncomfortable.''

"But—"

"No buts," he said, sliding open one of the doors and leading her into his bedroom. "The shower's through there." He pointed to a door. "There's shampoo and a hair dryer and anything else you might need." Opening the doors to a walk-in closet, he took out a silk lounging robe. "Here," he said, handing it to her, "you can use this. If you wash out your suit before you shower, you can throw it in the dryer that's just off the bathroom."

He seemed to have everything worked out, she thought, then shrugged. What the heck? When would she ever again get the chance to have supper cooked by the one and only Ryan St. James? "All right," she said. "You're on."

"Great. When you're finished, come on down to the kitchen."

"How will I find it?"

"Just follow your nose, lady," he said, grinning, then closed the door behind him.

She stared at the closed door, thinking about him. She couldn't help it; she liked him. There was something very attractive about Ryan, and it wasn't just his looks. In the pool, he hadn't forced himself on her. He'd just been alone with her in his bedroom, yet hadn't tried to wangle her into his bed. Suddenly she realized that she kept comparing him to Geoff.

She remembered being invited to Geoff's house for one dreadful weekend. He'd snuck into her room and refused to be put off, even when she whispered that she couldn't sleep with him under his parents' roof. He'd overcome her objections and they'd made love, then he'd sat by the next day, unblinking, as his mother informed Cass of Geoff's upcoming engagement.

"Sheila's such a *sweet* girl," Mrs. Sutton had said. "She and Geoff grew up together. You can see, can't you, Cass dear, that you're really not . . ." She'd trailed off, looking pained, trying to find the right words. Cass really couldn't hate the woman. She'd been almost gentle with Cass, trying to comfort her in what little ways she could.

Then Cass recalled her insight at the pool. Perhaps she'd obstinately directed her hatred at the rich these past five years, when money had nothing to do with it. Maybe the problem really had to do with the kind of person Geoff was. Cass jerked her thoughts away. That was a period of her life that she didn't care to remember.

She looked around Ryan's bedroom, noting the king-sized bed with its rust and white quilt, the carved wooden bookcases, the soft leather couch, the state-of-the-art stereo and television equipment.

Had Ryan really started out slinging hash at a seedy hamburger joint? Looking around his bedroom, she couldn't believe it. But what if her assumptions about Ryan were all wrong? What if his family wasn't wealthy, or his money inherited? What if he'd started out just like her and worked his way to the top?

She frowned, bewildered by the questions, which suddenly demanded answers. She'd gotten by quite nicely these past five years by organizing her life around one guiding principle: if you had money, you were no good. Now she was faced with the realization that she might not have been fair, or entirely honest with herself.

Absently, she rubbed Ryan's silk dressing gown against her cheek, then walked thoughtfully toward the bathroom. Someday, she'd have to sit down and give all this some thought. Wouldn't it be ironic if she'd been fighting her attraction to Ryan for all the wrong reasons? Maybe she didn't even need to fight it at all.

She came to a stop in the doorway that led to the bathroom, and looked down at the dressing gown she held in her hands. It was of the finest maroon silk, with black lapels and Ryan's initials embroidered in black on the pocket. Slowly, she traced her fingertip over the intertwined initials.

Taking a deep breath, she hung the garment on the back of the door and pulled the rubber band from her wet hair. Ryan was waiting for her, and if she didn't hurry, supper would be cold by the time she found her way to the kitchen.

Six

Cass wandered down the long corridor and came to the entrance hall, which soared three stories to a skylight in the cathedral ceiling. Looking up, she saw that dark clouds had completely covered the sun. It would rain before too long, and mercifully put an end to the unbearable heat. Not that Ryan would notice the heat—his entire house was comfortably air-conditioned.

She turned left and crossed through the living room, then came to a stop at the steps that led to the sunken dining room. Cass simply stared. The entire south wall was glass, facing the deck and the rolling meadows beyond, and underfoot there was a richly patterned oriental carpet. The table was elegantly set for two with a crystal bowl filled with daylilies serving as the centerpiece for the sumptuous display of sterling and china.

She was entranced by the room as it was; she didn't need the delicious aroma emanating from behind the door that presumably led to the kitchen. She grinned to herself. Ryan had been right—all she had to do to find the kitchen was follow her nose.

Pushing open the door, she found herself in the most modern kitchen she'd ever seen. No unsightly hardware marred its clean, spare lines and there was a round table set in a glassed-in greenhouse opening onto the wrap-around deck.

Ryan was chopping vegetables at a butcher-block island that seemed to fill the center of the room. He still wore his swim trunks and shirt, which, she noticed thankfully, he'd buttoned halfway. She didn't need more of his fantastic body to distract her. As it was, she was having enough trouble keeping her eyes off his legs.

"I'm impressed," she teased. "I expected to come in here and find a maid doing everything."

His blue eyes gleamed at her as he popped a snow pea into his mouth. "Uh-uh, I do it all—cook, clean, and wait tables." He shoved the vegetables aside and washed and dried his hands. "I even make drinks. What can I get you?"

"Do you have any white wine?"

"White wine," he said, taking a bottle from the refrigerator and finding a corkscrew. "Coming up."

He poured her a glass, then raised his beer in a toast. "To happiness."

"I'll drink to that," she said, smiling.

"While you're drinking to happiness, I'm going to sneak off and take a quick shower. Be right back."

"But—" She suddenly felt helpless. She wasn't used to being waited on. "Can't I at least do something while you're gone?"

"Well." He looked around. "I guess you could throw a salad together if you want."

"I think I can handle that."

He didn't answer right away; he just looked at her, his eyes filled with warmth. Then he said, "Be right back. Don't even think about leaving."

She shook her head, feeling goose bumps prickle up and down her arms. "I won't leave," she said.

He leaned over and kissed her softly. "Good," he murmured. "'Cause I'd only come after you if you did."

Then he was gone, and she was staring after him, bemused. The man should take out a patent on kissing—he had his technique down perfect.

Angry clouds were boiling on the horizon and thunder was rumbling ominously when Ryan returned. "We're in for it," he said, walking through the door. "If we're lucky, this heat wave will break before the night's out."

Cass looked up from the salad she was making. He'd changed into jeans and a white shirt with the sleeves rolled up, his hair still damp from his shower. "I hope whatever's in the oven smelling so good gets done before we lose electricity," she said.

"Be done in about five minutes," he said, sniffing appreciatively. "And even if the lights do go out, we're dining by candlelight, so nothing will be ruined."

"What *are* we having?"

"A surprise." He scooped the vegetables into a skillet and began to expertly stir-fry them. "The nutrients aren't lost if you steam or stir-fry vegetables," he said over his shoulder, "so I hope you like them this way."

Cass laughed. "Why's the man who single-handedly supplies more fat and cholesterol to the American diet worrying about nutrients?"

Ryan turned to look at her. "Is that what you think? That I'm ruining the average American's diet with Burger City food?"

She shrugged. "Aren't you?"

"No. We use a good quality meat, with less fat than the average ground beef, and we're experimenting with using whole grain breads and lower calorie dressings." He frowned. "When I started in this business eighteen years ago, I didn't know a damn thing about food. I just threw a burger on the grill and cooked it. Now, of course, we try to serve high quality meals but still keep the costs down, which is next to impossible. We can't get good help anymore and our costs rise every time the consumer's does."

"Then maybe you shouldn't have started meddling in the chicken business," Cass said lightly.

"Is that really why you profess to not like me, Cass? Because I'm competing with your business?"

She hesitated to answer. She felt so foolish telling him that she'd resented his success, and therefore had resented him. Finally she said, "I guess I made a lot of assumptions about you, Ryan."

"Such as?"

"Oh . . ." She shrugged. "I guess I had you pegged as an insufferable rich boy who'd been handed everything on a silver platter."

He laughed quietly and Cass saw that he was genuinely amused. "No, Cass," he said, smiling. "I started out as poor as they come." His smile faded as he searched her eyes and added gently, "Even poorer than you, I'm afraid."

It was her time to laugh, but there was no amusement in it. "I can't believe that, Ryan. *No* one is poorer than me!"

"Wealth isn't measured solely by money, you know," he said softly.

She cocked her head. "What do you mean?"

"I'll tell you sometime," he said, holding out his hand to her. "But now let's have dinner."

How did one keep from falling in love? Cass mused. Dinner was perfect, a lobster casserole with wild rice, stir-fried vegetables, the tossed salad she'd made and wine. Afterward, when the storm hit and the lights flickered and then went out, Ryan lit a fire in the fireplace and they sat on the long white couch and talked, oblivious to the raging storm outside. Somehow the subject came around again to her misconceptions about him.

"You thought I'd be into wild nightlife and all sorts of illicit activities, eh?" he asked, smiling.

"Well, face it, Ryan—you *are* a workaholic. You admit it yourself. Men on the fast track sometimes are taken in by the trappings of money."

He nodded thoughtfully. "Yes, though for me, it's never been money per se that's important. It's what money symbolizes."

"Which is?"

"Power. Being in control. Holding the upper hand." He frowned. "I suppose admitting that makes me smaller in your eyes."

"It depends on who you want power over," she said slowly.

"My destiny, of course," he answered. "I don't have any desire to run the world, Cass. I just want to be in control of my *own* world."

"I see. . . ." She gazed into the fireplace, troubled. That's what everyone wanted, she supposed—to be in control of his or her own destiny, not to feel helpless, at the mercy of others. It's certainly what *she* wanted, so in that respect, she could understand Ryan St. James.

But could she ever love a man like that, one driven so much to succeed that he never took vacations, and gave his life totally to his business? Every woman knew she'd have to share her man with his job, but every woman wanted to think that she was at least as important as his occupation. Would any woman ever be that important to Ryan St. James? Wouldn't the woman in Ryan's life be given small moments here and there, then forgotten?

Cass frowned. She wasn't the kind of person who'd marry a wealthy man just for the financial security, and be happy to let him devote his life elsewhere. She wanted a real marriage, based on love. She wanted to share her husband's life and dreams and problems, and she wanted a man who would be willing to share hers, too. Unless she missed her guess, Ryan St. James wasn't that man.

"You're being very quiet," Ryan said.

She looked at him, startled. She'd almost forgotten where she was, who she was with. "Yes," she said. "I was thinking."

"Are you going to tell me what about?"

She lifted solemn eyes to his. "I was thinking how different we are."

"How do you know?" he asked. "You don't even know me. You yourself admitted that you had me figured for a spoiled rich boy, when that's the farthest thing from the truth. Why don't you give yourself a chance to get to know me, not just make up your mind based on what you think I am?"

"You're persistent, aren't you?" she asked, smiling despite herself.

"Very," he murmured, reaching out to touch a strand of her hair. "Cass, I think you'll find that we're a lot alike, you and I."

She laughed and shook her head. "We're like night and day."

"Which, when you think about it, go together. You can't have one without the other...."

She felt warm inside, and knew that she wanted to see him again. It had been a long time since she'd been this attracted to a man, a long time since she'd experienced this pleasurable heightening of her senses. "All right," she said. "I'll give you a chance." She laughed musically. "I'll stay until this storm is over. Think you can convince me how nice you are in thirty minutes?"

His eyes seemed to be heated by banked fires. "I think I could convince you of a lot of things in thirty minutes," he murmured.

Suddenly, his voice was lower, more intense. Cass shivered as he traced a soft line down her cheek with his finger, then paused at the corner of her lips. She couldn't look away from his eyes; they held her as surely as a net captures a butterfly. Then it was too late to back away—he was lowering his head as if in slow motion and she was lifting her face to his, experiencing the incredible rush of anticipation. His lips gently brushed hers, lifted, then came down on hers again, harder this time, more demanding. His tongue probed her mouth and her lips parted and then she was in his arms, caught up in the magic of body against body, heat against heat.

"Oh, Cass," he breathed raggedly when their lips parted. "You feel so good." His eyes searched hers. "It's never been like this before, Cass. Do you feel it, too?"

She nodded. "Yes, but it—" She broke off. She was afraid to tell him what she was feeling, afraid to admit she was afraid.

"It what?" he urged in a low voice. "Is there someone else?"

She shook her head. "No."

"Was there once?"

She hesitated. "Yes, but that was years ago. I'm over him now."

He studied her. "Are you sure, Cass? Is he the reason you don't want to get involved with me?"

"I..." She frowned. She didn't want to talk about Geoff, didn't even know what she felt anymore. She needed time to think before she could speak plainly. Abruptly, she stood up. "I think I'd better go, Ryan."

He sat looking up at her, his eyes heated with intensity, then he slowly shook his head. "No," he said softly, and reached out and took her hand. "I'm not letting you get away that easily. Come back to me."

Gently, he tugged on her hand. She tried to resist, but everything in her seemed to yearn toward him. She sank onto the couch, her entire body filled with the drumming of her heart, the insistent pulsing in her veins. She realized then how dishonest she'd been with herself—she'd pretended not to like Ryan, when all along she'd been so attracted to him she couldn't think straight. From now on, she vowed, she was going to follow her heart, the devil with logic.

His touch made it easy for her. He took her in his arms and dropped feather-light kisses on her face, her closed eyelids, her cheeks and forehead. He murmured to her, his voice a deep, low rumble in his throat. He moved his hands sensuously over her back, pulling her closer to him, enclosing her in his potent embrace.

Everything was sensation. Unleashed from the narrow confines of fear, her body blossomed. She felt as if she were filled with light. She trembled, but didn't fight the sensations that shook her. Then she wasn't just receiving Ryan's caresses any longer, she was giving them back without reserve. Her lips seemed expert in their knowledge as she kissed the sensitive cords in his strong neck. She caressed his back, trailing her fingertips down the rippling muscles and then around to his ribs and chest and the flat expanse of his stomach.

She delighted when she heard his low groan of pleasure, then thrilled when he took her hand and placed it inside his shirt and held it against his pounding heart.

"This is what you do to me, Cass," he murmured, his lips torturing her with fiery kisses. "My heart isn't mine anymore; it's like a madman, pounding in my chest, wanting you...."

She moaned softly and put her arms around his neck, drawing his head down. She kissed him measure for measure, tongue against tongue, probing, circling, crazed with desire.

"I want to touch you, Cass," he whispered, pressing hot kisses into her hair, down to her ear, along the sensitive skin of her neck. "I want to feel your skin against mine, your breasts in my hands. Tell me you want it, too."

Oh, but he knew how to drive a woman mad! "Yes," she breathed raggedly. "Yes...please."

Slowly, expertly, as if they had all the time in the world, he put his hand under her T-shirt, caressing her back lightly as he found the clasp of her bathing suit top. He fumbled only for a moment, then the top was undone and she felt it loosen, her breasts aching with anticipation and her nipples tightening into tiny insistent pebbles.

"Oh, Cass," he murmured as he covered her breasts with his hands. "Dear Cass..."

She moaned and pressed her body against his, craving the feel of his palms cupping her breasts, massaging slowly, erotically, caressing in ever-widening, ever-demanding circles. Her body felt on fire and her nipples were hard and urgent in his hands. She ran her hands up and down his back, her eyes closed, her head thrown back as his lips traveled in sensual pathways down her neck to the hollow of her throat. But it wasn't enough; her body cried out for more, demanded more. The need was a pulsing inside her, urging her on.

"Don't stop," she whispered. "Please, Ryan, kiss me."

He groaned and pulled her T-shirt over her head—slipping the bikini top off at the same time—and he laid her back against the pillows on the couch. In slow seduction, he trailed teasing kisses down her throat to the hollow between her breasts as he brushed his thumbs erotically back and forth against her swollen nipples, coaxing, urging, demanding her response.

She thought she might explode from the drumming need, but at last he touched his lips to her breasts, teasing one with soft kisses, driving her mad with need. He was the lover she'd always envisioned, slow and gentle yet wonderfully passionate, holding back until she thought she might explode, then giving her everything she wanted and more.

She hugged him tightly, her eyes squeezed shut in ecstasy. She began to tremble when he parted his lips and slowly caressed her nipple with his tongue. Stars seemed to dance behind her closed eyelids and rockets soared in the black night of her mind. She felt her back arching, felt herself falling into steamy desire, felt her hips begin a slow, rhythmic motion against his. She was simply Woman, he Man. There were no rules, no conventions, only this enormous desire flaming between them, urging them to completion. If ever there were anything right in life, this was it.

But somehow, even when she'd lost all ability to think, Ryan was still in control. He lifted his head and looked down at her. Slowly, she opened her eyes. "I want to make love with you, Cass," he said, "but I want it to be right for you."

She stared into his eyes, caught in a quandary. Her body was urging her on, but a tiny doubt flickered in her mind. She'd never given herself to a man she didn't love, and while she knew she had a right to physical pleasure, she also knew that *making* love was not the same as loving. Slowly, she sat up. "I want to make love with you, too," she finally said softly, "but now isn't the time. Not yet, anyway." She drew her T-shirt on, then searched his eyes. "Are you angry with me for stopping?"

He shook his head, his eyes like dark sapphires in the firelight. "Of course not," he said, smiling and taking her hand. "If I didn't want to give you a choice, I wouldn't have stopped and asked you. Right now, I could have been making love to you, not watching you sit there, all covered up and looking shy and entirely too beautiful for your own good."

She felt herself relax, felt her smile grow in response to his. "I appreciate your asking, Ryan, more than I can ever tell you."

He began to toy with her hair. "You're special, Cass," he finally said. "I'm not going to insist on anything you're still unsure about. I want you to want it as much as I do—with no doubts."

She stared at him, not knowing what to think. "You're not playing the game right," she said at last. "Most men would take what they could get and forget about trying for more."

"Some things, Cass," he said softly, "are more important than momentary pleasures."

Yes, she thought sadly, some things were—like freedom, for one. Ryan St. James wouldn't be interested in getting involved and settling down with a poor girl from Waterbury. She had nothing to offer him—she didn't come from a wealthy family, didn't have the right kind of background to make her a suitable wife. But she wouldn't sleep with him, then stand by and watch him drive away tomorrow morning, never to see him again. She might not have lots of money, but she was rich with pride.

She stood up. "I'm afraid it's time for me to leave." She glanced toward the deck, where rain pounded against the glass doors like a terrified child seeking shelter. "Thank you for dinner. It really was lovely."

He sat looking up at her, frowning. "Something's wrong," he said thoughtfully. "Suddenly, I've lost you. What happened? What did I say to upset you?"

"You didn't say anything," she said lightly. "Really, I've just got to go."

"At least stay until this storm is over," he urged, standing up. "You'll get drenched the minute you step out in this."

"I won't melt," she said lightly, swinging her long hair deftly over her shoulders and turning toward the hall.

At the door, she turned back to him. She was determined not to let him kiss her again, so she kissed him quickly on the cheek, a profoundly sisterly peck, then she opened the door and sprinted out into the rain. "Good night, Ryan," she called over her shoulder.

"Cass," Ryan shouted, "for crying out loud, at least let me give you an umbrella or coat...."

"Too late now," she called back, hoping her voice sounded happy. "See you."

Ryan stood in the doorway, staring moodily at the red taillights on her car until they disappeared around the curve of the driveway. Slowly, he closed the door and walked into the living room and stood with his hands in his pockets, staring out at the rain. It pounded against the doors, splashed and clattered on the wooden deck, drummed on the roof. In the fireplace, the logs shifted and the fire momentarily flared, then settled into a gentle crackling.

Turning, Ryan looked at the couch, and the memory of
her skin came back to him. He groaned softly and turned
away. Memories like that would keep him from sleeping all
night. Cass had been right—he shouldn't have been so gallant. Some things weren't meant to be denied. He frowned
and thought about tomorrow. He had to drive back to the
city. As usual, his desk would be piled high with projects
and reports. Yet for the first time in memory, he wasn't
looking forward to work. He found himself staring at the
couch, remembering Cass, how her skin had felt under his
lips and hands.

Ryan bit off an expletive and headed for his study. He'd
get no sleep tonight; perhaps he could work on that report
he'd brought with him.

Seven

On Monday, Cass told herself she'd done the only sensible thing. Meeting Ryan St. James had been a fluke and she'd never see him again. It was foolish to even think of getting involved with a man like him.

Meanwhile, Ryan drove back to New York and missed his exit because he'd been thinking of Cass. He frowned and cursed his stupidity and told himself to get his mind back on business, where it belonged.

On Tuesday, Cass found herself smiling dreamily all day as she went over and over what had happened between them. She burned an entire batch of chicken and Henry said he'd take it out of her share of the profits. She vowed to never think of Ryan St. James again.

In New York, Ryan found himself staring into space a lot, unable to concentrate. Every report he tried to read was dry and boring. Searching through his Rolodex, he couldn't find the name of even one woman he wanted to call and he

cursed himself again when he realized he didn't even know
Cass's number.

On Wednesday, Cass woke up panic-stricken; she couldn't
remember what Ryan looked like. She lay in bed and closed
her eyes. Concentrating very hard, she still couldn't see him.
She threw back the covers and paced agitatedly around her
bedroom but she got only glimpses of his face. On her way
to work that morning, while she was stopped at the same
traffic light where Ryan had asked her to go bowling, his
face came back to her, as clearly as if she were looking at his
photograph. She felt an enormous peace come over her.
Silly, but somehow, remembering what he looked like comforted her. Hours later, when she realized she'd never see
him again, she stopped being comforted and wished she had
it all to do over again. *This* time, she wouldn't be so stupid.

That same morning, Ryan lay in bed and stared at the
ceiling. He had a nine o'clock conference that he couldn't
care less about—he was thinking about Cass. He saw her in
vivid detail—how she'd looked in that silly chicken outfit,
with her long legs flashing spiritedly in the sun; how she'd
looked in her jeans and T-shirt, in her skimpy bikini—out
of her skimpy bikini... He groaned and catapulted out of
bed, dashed into the shower and sang at the top of his lungs.
But nothing worked; she was still firmly lodged in his mind
when he sat in the conference room, trying to concentrate on
the driest presentation he'd ever heard in his life.

On Thursday, Cass met a man at the laundromat. He was
tall, with a great body, curly hair, and a nice grin. His name
was Harry. She realized she might have found him enor-
mously attractive if she hadn't just spent a week thinking
about Ryan St. James. Harry asked her out, but she smiled
and shook her head. He grinned. "Got a boyfriend already, eh?" Remembering Ryan, she nodded. "Yeah," she
said, smiling. "I do....," she said, wishing it was true.

That afternoon, Ryan called Patricia Hollings. She was a model whose face had graced the cover of several fashion magazines over the past few years and who he'd dated sporadically for over a year. That night, they went out for dinner. As Patricia prattled on and on about her shoot that day, Ryan looked around at the restaurant's decor and thought for the first time how pretentious it was to have latticework in a Manhattan restaurant, as if the gardenlike setting could hide the fact that they were in a noisy, dirty city. He suddenly wished he was in Woodbury, out on the deck looking over the rolling meadows, feeling the good, clean country air in his lungs, looking at Cass...

"Ryan?" Patricia Hollings said, frowning. "Are you listening?"

"Hmm?"

"I asked if you were listening, darling." She relaxed into her famous smile. "You're not, are you? You're thinking about business again, aren't you?"

"Business?" he repeated blankly, then gathered his wits and nodded. It was easier that way. How could he explain Cass to Patricia Hollings when he couldn't even explain her to himself?

On Friday, Cass stood in the steaming kitchen of Chick-O-Rama, making a batch of cole slaw and staring glumly into the future. She'd grow old in this furnace of a kitchen. She'd get fat and her hair would turn gray and she'd have to start wearing orthopedic shoes, and she'd *still* remember last weekend and the time she spent with Ryan St. James.

"You sick, Cass?" Henry asked when he entered the kitchen. It was two o'clock and they were about to change shifts.

"No." She put another plastic lid on a pint container of cole slaw. "I'm fine, Henry. Why?"

"Because you're not fine," Henry answered, frowning as he studied her. Then he nodded, breaking into a huge smile. "You're in love."

She almost dropped the ten containers of cole slaw she was carrying to the built-in refrigerator. *"What?"* she said. "What are you talking about?"

"I'm talking about love," Henry said, grinning. "L-O-V-E."

"You don't have to spell it for me, Henry," she said. "I *know* what the heck it is."

"Uh-huh," he said, tying an apron around his expansive middle. "I know you do. So you gonna tell me about him?"

"About who?" she asked irritably.

"About the guy who done this to you."

"No guy *done* this to me, Henry," she said, shaking her head at him and widening her eyes. "You're just a silly old bachelor, so you think everyone else on earth is thinking about L-O-V-E, as you call it, just like you."

"I had my chance to settle down, you know, Cass," Henry said affably.

Cass stared at him momentarily. "You did? When?"

"Oh, God, thirty years ago now. I was a good-looking young buck, you know." He tapped his ample stomach. "Didn't have this then either. The women adored me."

"Yeah?" Cass smiled to herself. Henry was such a dear. Since he'd never shared much of his personal history with her, she found herself curious. "So what happened?"

"Agh!" Henry waved a gnarled hand. "I was a jerk. She wanted to get married and I wanted my freedom. I was a typical male."

He kept talking, but Cass wasn't listening anymore. She was thinking about Ryan. Would he stand in the board-room of his Burger City empire some day telling a niece that he regretted not having settled down? Would he even *remember* Cass in thirty years?

"Hey," Henry said. "Are you listening?"

"Huh?" She snapped out of her reverie. "Oh, I'm sorry, Henry, I got sidetracked. So why didn't you go after her later?"

"I tried," he said, and suddenly he wasn't grinning anymore. He looked old and sad and Cass felt her heart swell with love for him. "Only trouble was, she found a man who *did* want to settle down, so she married him and had a couple kids." He shook his head as he stared thoughtfully into the past. "That was the biggest mistake I ever made."

"I'm sorry, Uncle Henry," Cass said softly.

He shook himself and smiled. "Thanks, kid. Nice to hear you call me Uncle for a change."

Laughing, she threw her balled-up apron at him and headed for the door. "Have fun this weekend, Henry," she called as she made her way through the front of the store. "This is my one weekend off this month, so I'm going to enjoy it."

"Got a date with your new honey?" he called after her.

"I haven't got a honey," she yelled over her shoulder as she opened the front door. "And I haven't got a date tonight either." Then she came to a thumping halt. Grinning at her not more than ten inches away was Ryan St. James.

"That's nice to know," he said, his blue eyes laughing. "Does that mean there's a chance for me?"

Cass couldn't speak—she could barely breathe. Happiness flooded her and goose bumps broke out over her arms. Somehow she managed to regain her composure, but it wasn't easy. "Maybe," she said flippantly, tossing her hair over a shoulder. "What'd you have in mind?"

"Dinner tonight," Ryan said. "Then maybe some dancing."

"I thought you were in New York."

"I was," he said. "But I realized I wanted to see you again, so I came back. So? Will you go out with me tonight?"

Would she go out with him? Would any woman in her right mind turn down an invitation from a man she'd dreamed about all week? Still, she wasn't about to act too thrilled. She shrugged casually. "Okay," she said. "I haven't got anything else to do."

They drove all the way to Hartford for dinner at a new restaurant, and Ryan ordered a bottle of wine that cost more than Cass spent on food in a month. They sat in the serenely elegant dining room until they were the only ones left, then, because they wanted to talk, they went to a dark cocktail lounge and listened to quiet jazz.

It was raining when they left and the sidewalks shimmered with reflections. They strolled arm in arm to Ryan's car, focused on each other, laughing at the gentle rain that misted them. As cars went by, tires whispered on the wet road and oil-slicked puddles magically turned into rainbows. The night air was cool and damp and tinged with the faint odor of hamburgers and fries from the all-night fastfood restaurant up the street.

At the car, Ryan took Cass in his arms and kissed her—a long, slow kiss that made her senses reel. She didn't want the kiss to end, so it didn't. She twined her arms around his neck and her body melted into his and his arms tightened around her. When they at last surfaced, Ryan groaned and rocked her back and forth.

"Lady," he sighed, kissing her temple, "how'm I gonna drive us home?"

She smiled. Her eyes were closed and her face was filled with dreamy rapture. "Do you want me to drive?"

"No," he breathed, kissing her eyelids. "I don't want either of us to drive. I want to make love with you."

"Here?" she asked, laughing throatily. She was having a wonderful time, but she was still cautious enough to make a joke out of his statement. "I thought all rational people made love in bed."

"Rational, smational," he said as he nuzzled her ear. "What does being rational have to do with making love?"

She widened her eyes in pretended innocence. "Doesn't everyone do a cost-benefit analysis before going to bed with someone?"

His eyes grew serious. "Cass," he said, "I'm not joking. I want to make love with you."

She swallowed hard. "I see," she said. "Well, I *was* joking a little."

He nodded, looking even more serious. "I know. That's what's bothering me." He ran his knuckles up and down her cheek, his eyes roaming her face. Then he took a deep breath. "Okay, I'll drive you home."

She put a hand on his arm. "I was only joking a little, Ryan."

His eyes seemed as dark as the midnight sky, his smile warmer than the sun. "Then in the next few days, I'm going to see if I can convince you to take me as seriously as I take you."

He kissed her good-night at her front door. "Aren't you going to come in for coffee?"

"No," he said. "If I went in, I'd want a lot more than coffee." He kissed her again. "Good night, Cass. I'll call you tomorrow. Maybe you could come out for a swim. We could have a cookout."

Cass squinted up into the mist that surrounded them like a nimbus. "You haven't been listening to the radio, Ryan," she said, smiling. "It's going to rain all weekend."

With a low groan, he pulled her against him. "The hell with the weather," he said. "This is what I want."

When she surfaced from the kiss, she was trembling. "I wish you'd come in for a while, Ryan," she whispered.

"Tomorrow," he said, kissing her hungrily.

She clung to him, shaking even harder. "Why tomorrow?" she asked between kisses.

"Because," he murmured, groaning as he ran his hands up and down her back.

"Because why?" she whispered.

He broke off the kiss. "Because I haven't got any protection with me, Cass," he said, looking her straight in the eye.

For a minute, she didn't understand. Then she did. "Oh."

He smiled and took her in his arms again. "I wish desire didn't carry such consequences." He sighed and rocked her back and forth, his chin resting on her head. "For the first time in my life, I'm tempted to take a chance."

She rubbed her cheek against his jacket, which felt warm and expensive. "You're a fine man, Ryan," she said softly.

Ryan looked troubled. "It's just as well we don't make love yet, Cass," he said. "We still need to get to know each other better."

She peered up at him, wondering what he meant. "It's refreshing to meet a man who wants to talk instead of tumble into bed." She went up on tiptoe and kissed him softly. "Good night, Ryan."

"Good night, Cass. I'll call in the morning."

Later, when she lay in bed, she realized Ryan wasn't a bit like Geoff. She had to face her past and come to terms with it, before she let it ruin her life. She groaned and turned on her side, remembering the weekend at Geoff's home. She'd been twenty years old. How could she have been so naive? She remembered excusing herself from the living room after Mrs. Sutton told her about Geoff's engagement, then lying on the bed in the guest room, sobbing as if her heart were broken. The door had opened and Geoff had come in. She remembered sitting up, still sobbing. Even then, she couldn't believe what had happened.

"Cass," Geoff had said, sitting on the edge of the bed and running a hand through her hair. "Don't cry, darling. It doesn't have to be over for us."

She remembered lifting her head, feeling perhaps everything would be all right. "You mean it?" she asked breathlessly. "You still want me?"

"Of course I want you," he said, his voice deepening. He ran his hand down her back to the swell of her hip. "I'll always want you, Cass."

"You'd go against your parents for me?" she asked, her eyes shining.

"My parents don't have to know," he crooned, beginning to unbutton her blouse. He dipped his head and kissed her roughly. "It'll always be you, Cass. Just you."

"But..." She tried to stop him, tried to keep his hand from going under her skirt.

"Cass," he breathed. "Don't talk. Let's just have sex."

She flinched. She hated it when he used that term. Why couldn't he say "make love"? She sat up and looked at him. "I *need* to talk, Geoff."

"And I need this," he said, smiling at her. "You turn me on, Cass. You always will."

"But how are we going to tell your parents? We can't just keep it from them. How can we be married—"

"Married?" He'd lain there, looking so incredibly handsome, with his blond hair falling into his blue eyes, his expensive shirt open at the collar, exposing his gold-toned skin. "Honey, I thought you understood. I'm going to marry Sheila."

She simply stared at him. "But . . ." She almost laughed. He had to be joking. "Geoff, you said you love me."

"I do, Cass," he said, running his hand up her arm. "Just because I marry Sheila doesn't mean I have to stop seeing you. Hell, we won't get married for at least another year or two, anyway. She'll want one of those long engagements, so she can have lots of parties and enjoy herself before settling down to being a dull old married woman." He'd chuckled sardonically. "Who knows? Maybe Sheila wants to have a last fling too."

She remembered staring at him, and then pushing him away, seeing him in a blinding flash of insight for what he was. She remembered feeling suddenly chilled. She'd gotten up and packed her bag, and their chauffeur had driven her home. All the way home, she'd sat silently, her mouth closed in a hard, firm line, her chin raised defensively. She'd vowed she would never, *never* have anything to do with anyone rich again.

Cass closed her eyes on the memory, remembering the pain, no longer trying to shut it out, seeing everything clearly at last. Money had nothing to do with it, she realized. It was just Geoff and his family. She'd fallen in love with a bum, a good-for-nothing heel, and to keep from facing the truth, she'd insisted on believing that anyone rich couldn't be trusted.

Feeling as if she'd climbed a mountain, she turned over and went to sleep, her face serene, her dreams at last untroubled.

The phone's shrill ring woke her from deep sleep. She fumbled for the receiver, dropped it, then sleepily reached over the side of the bed and fished around for it. "H'lo?" she mumbled when she at last retrieved it.

Ryan's deep voice came intimately over the receiver, sending chills through her and waking her up completely. "Are you still in bed?"

"Mmm-hmm," she said, lying back and cradling the phone on her pillow. A soft smile trembled at her lips.

Ryan groaned. "I've got to do something about my imagination," he said. "It's driving me crazy right now."

Her smile grew. "What are you imagining?"

"You," he said, sounding a little hoarse. "In bed. With some sexy black nightie on."

She laughed musically. "Picture this: me, in bed, wearing a ratty old pair of sweatpants and a sweatshirt."

"You still look good enough to have for lunch."

"Lunch? What about breakfast?"

"At eleven-thirty?" he asked, chuckling.

"Are you kidding?" She sat up, scraped her hair back from her eyes, and peered at the alarm clock. "I can't believe it! I never sleep this late."

"Must have been a late night."

She smiled and rested her chin on her knees, toying with the phone cord. "Yeah, matter of fact, it was."

"I'd like to keep you out even later tonight, Cass."

"Would you?" She closed her eyes and took a tremulous breath. She felt all fluttery inside, filled with sweet anticipation.

"Actually," he said, "I'd like to spend the whole day with you. Why don't I pick you up for lunch in a half an hour?"

"Make it an hour and you've got a deal."

"Done."

When Ryan arrived a little after twelve-thirty, she was ready. She wore a pair of white trousers and a white blouse, and carried a navy slicker to ward off the rain. Her hair was done in a neat chignon at the back of her neck. Ryan escorted her to his low-slung sports car, then got in, but instead of starting the engine, he took her in his arms.

"I didn't sleep much last night," he said huskily, brushing his lips insistently against hers. "I spent most of the night thinking about you."

She clung to him, shivering under the onslaught of his nearness. "Oh? I'm sorry to hear that."

"I'm not sorry," he murmured as he nibbled at her earlobe. "I'd go without sleep and food for a week if I could hold you like this during that time."

She stared into his eyes. "Maybe we'd better have some lunch," she suggested. It was that or lose her head right here in his car in the middle of her driveway. She could just imagine what the neighbors would think!

He sighed and, releasing her, started the engine. "You're a hard woman, Cass Dickens," he said, shaking his head as he maneuvered the car onto the road. "What am I going to do with you?"

She laughed musically. "Why don't you have lunch with me?"

"Sounds great. Got any place special in mind?"

She shook her head and scrunched down in the luxurious leather bucket seat. "Nope, let's just drive until we find a likely place."

They talked so much, they didn't even realize where they were until they arrived in Salisbury, in the northwest corner of the state. They ate a late lunch in a charming inn, then sat drinking coffee, in no hurry to leave. Wind slashed at the trees and chased leaves along the lawn. The rain battered against the panes and the windows shook, but inside all was comfortable and the waiters didn't seem to mind them staying. They ordered liqueurs and settled down in the comfortable living room in front of a roaring fireplace.

"Did you really start out slinging hash in a greasy spoon?" Cass asked.

Ryan laughed. "I started on the grill at Billy Bob Sawyer's hamburger joint in the small town in Texas where I grew up. I won't even tell you how much I got paid—it was barely enough to keep me in milk shakes and root beer for the week."

She shook her head. "I can't see you like that. It doesn't fit, somehow. What happened? How did you get from there to here?"

He looked around, as if seeing more than the room where they sat. "I have a theory about success," he said, looking back at her. "To get it, you have to be hungry."

"Hungry?"

"Yeah. It's like a burning inside you. The hunger acts like a fuel and pushes you to go beyond what anyone expected of you or what you even expected of yourself, because you *have* to succeed. Because if you didn't, it would be almost like you didn't exist."

She looked into his eyes and saw the hunger he was talking about and it almost frightened her, because she sensed too well what he was talking about, knew the same gnawing desire to better herself. Maybe Ryan was right; maybe they were a lot alike. "But how did you make the leap from working on the grill to owning it?"

Ryan stretched his long legs toward the fire and smiled as if to himself. "It's a long story. I dropped out of school when I was sixteen and joined the army. I was full of myself—cocky and arrogant, brash. You'd have hated me!" Cass smiled and he continued. "They knocked the living daylights out of me though. I did more KP than any raw recruit in the history of the entire army, I think. But there's one good thing you can say for the armed forces—they teach you to be a man. They kicked all that out of me and in the meantime, I put every cent I earned those four years in the bank. When I got out, I had a tidy sum saved up. But I didn't have any plans, didn't even know what I wanted to do with my life, so I went back home to visit my mother.''

He stopped talking, his eyes turned inward as if he were remembering. A smile touched his lips and he continued. ''Well, maybe it was just fate. When I got home, I found out Billy Bob had fallen on hard times. He'd put his burger place on the market and I had some money, so I decided to give it a whirl. I got a bank loan and bought Billy Bob's Burgers and changed the name to Burger City, and the rest is history.''

''But that's just the beginning, Ryan! Why wasn't one burger place in a small town enough for you? What made *you* be the one in a million who goes on to such tremendous success? I mean, there are thousands of guys who save up money in the army and go back home and open a business and they're content to live the rest of their lives in some little town....'' She trailed off, looking into his eyes. ''What makes you different, Ryan?'' she asked softly.

He chuckled sardonically. ''What makes Ryan run, eh?''

''Exactly.''

''It's that hunger, Cass. Some of us have it and some of us don't. I couldn't have been content to stay in that one-horse town. It would have been a living death for me. I needed to get out.'' He shrugged. ''So I did. I just kept growing and growing and one day Texas wasn't big enough to hold me; I needed the entire country.''

And what would a man like Ryan St. James want now? Cass wondered. One day, even this country might be too small for him. There was something frightening about so much ambition, and then she realized it was because it came from such great need. What had happened to Ryan to cause this hunger? And was there any way in the world to feed it, or was he doomed to eternal dissatisfaction, to a never-ending lust for more?

It was ironic, but Cass found herself wishing Ryan was the man she'd originally thought he was—a man with inherited wealth, secure in himself and his position. That kind of man would be easier to get to know. He would have no new worlds to conquer and might even be ready to settle down. But a man like Ryan might never lose the need to prove himself, and he would probably never succumb to the desire to settle down.

They left the inn at five o'clock and headed home, and Ryan continued to talk. It was as if a dam had burst and all the words he'd bottled up were coming out. Cass sat back and listened, knowing instinctively that he was telling her more than he'd ever told anyone else.

"I've never had any regrets about my work," he said slowly. "You hear about people stuck in jobs they hate, but I can't even begin to imagine what that's like."

"Perhaps that's part of the secret of your success, Ryan," Cass said. "All your energy goes into what you love, instead of into wishing you were doing something else."

"You might be right, though that's not it entirely. When I was a kid, I was the town's outcast. I never fit in and was always getting into trouble—a real 'rebel without a cause.' I always felt as if it were just me and my mom against the world."

"What about your dad?" Cass asked. That was the second time Ryan had mentioned his mother without talking about his father. She didn't want to pry, but somehow she thought it was important.

"He died before I was born."

"I see," Cass said slowly. "Your mother never remarried?"

"No," he said, taking her hand. "She lives in a big, brick house outside of Dallas." He smiled. "She's happy. I've made sure she's financially secure for life and she says she's even found a man she might be interested in marrying."

"How do you feel about that?"

He smiled easily. "It's what I've wanted for her all my life. I hope she does marry the guy. It'll be the best thing that ever happened to her." His smile faded. "Lord knows, she had a rotten time most of her life."

Cass had turned in the seat to face Ryan. "In what way?" she asked gently.

"About every way there was," he said, eyes straight ahead. "Financially, romantically..." He shook his head. "Nothing much went right for her for years, and I didn't make it any easier. It's not easy to raise a kid by yourself anytime, but in those days it was even harder. She worked in a hardware store for a while, then became a beautician." He fell silent for a moment, his face set. "She did women's hair and got a lousy quarter tip and then had to put up with my getting into trouble at school, on the streets..." He shook his head. "She's a fine woman. She deserves a hell of a lot more from life than she got."

"So that's where the hunger comes from," Cass said softly.

Suddenly it was almost too quiet in the car. "Not completely, Cass," he said tiredly. "Though that's some of it. But I'm not so altruistic that I've spent my life pursuing success just because I wanted my mother to have more in life. No, the hunger's mine. When I was a kid, it burned in me like fire. I was angry all the time, wanting to prove myself to others, wanting to show them who I was."

"Is that why you work so hard? To prove yourself?"

"Not anymore," he said slowly. "I've been lucky. I was able to work the anger out and come to terms with it. But for a long time..." He shook his head. "For a long time, that's what it was. I worked hard so I could get back at everyone, for every time some kid in town had called me a bastard."

"When I was a kid, I wore glasses," she said, smiling. "Everyone called me 'four eyes.' God! How I hated that." She frowned. "It's strange how things that happen in your childhood stay with you all your life."

Ryan tightened his hands on the steering wheel. "Yeah," he said shortly. "Isn't it though?"

Cass stared at his hands and saw how tightly he gripped the wheel. Thoughtfully, she lifted her gaze to his face. He was frowning, his eyebrows low over his eyes, deep ridges cutting grooves into his face as he stared at the road ahead. Part of her wanted to reach out and touch him, but some instinct told her not to.

Cass turned her head to look out the window at the passing countryside, wondering what it would take for a man like Ryan St. James to open up completely and allow himself to be vulnerable.

Eight

———

"Good grief," Cass said, staring at the aqua water, "you really *do* have an indoor pool."

"Of course," Ryan said, eyes gleaming mischievously. "Doesn't everyone?"

She teetered on the edge of laughter, then gave in. "Oh, Ryan," she said, putting her arms around him. "I was such a goose! I was so busy hating you because you had money I couldn't even think straight."

"Well, it *is* a minor character flaw," he teased, "but I think I can put up with it."

"I wasn't always like this, you know," she said slowly. "I mean, I didn't grow up hating the rich because Dad and I didn't have much money. In fact, I don't remember ever thinking about money when I was growing up. I was really pretty happy and well-adjusted."

"So this is an aberration acquired in your adult life, eh?" Ryan asked, putting on a thick German accent and twirling an imaginary moustache, squeezing one eye shut as if he were peering through a monocle.

Cass burst out laughing and hugged him hard, her eyes shining. Every minute she spent with Ryan showed her a new facet of him. His sense of humor was what she liked best about him, and he had the nicest way of gently teasing her out of her silly fears and prejudices.

He hugged her back, then rested his chin atop her head. "I'm glad you decided to give me a chance, Cass," he said, his tone suddenly serious.

She kept her cheek nestled against his chest, fighting with herself. She didn't have to tell him anything about Geoff. What had happened between them was over and done with. Didn't advice columnists always counsel that discretion was more important than complete honesty? Anyway, she didn't have anything to confess. It wasn't as if *she'd* been the one to lead Geoff on.

"Cass?" Ryan tilted her chin up with a gentle finger and peered into her face. "You okay?"

She debated only a moment, then shook her head. "You deserve to know why I was so against you in the beginning, Ryan."

His face grew serious. "I see. Are you sure you really want to tell me?"

Unable to answer, she walked to the edge of the pool. It was like something out of the pages of a Hollywood movie magazine. On the lowest level of the house, with a wall of windows overlooking the gentle roll of meadows backed by forest, the pool was surrounded by towering indoor plants and trees. Yellow-cushioned chaise lounges sat on the flagstone floor. She stood looking at it all, knowing she wanted to tell Ryan about Geoff, but not knowing how. It didn't bother her to admit that Geoff had dumped her, but she was terribly ashamed of how she'd reacted by turning against

everyone that could possibly be like him. Her response had
been irrational, and she didn't like admitting her faults.

Taking a deep breath, she turned around. "You see, I
used to date a guy a few years back..."

"Ah," Ryan said, nodding knowingly. "So there *is* another man in the picture."

"Will you stop teasing?" she said, laughing despite herself, then feeling grateful. Ryan knew exactly how to handle her; by making jokes about what she was so reluctant to
discuss, he helped her relax.

"I'm sorry," he said quietly, not teasing now. "Go ahead,
Cass. I didn't mean to make fun of what you're saying."

"I know that, Ryan," she said, smiling at him and feeling even more grateful. He knew exactly when to joke and
tease, but even more important, he knew when not to. "It
was over five years ago, actually. I was a student at Yale and
I—"

"You went to Yale?" Ryan stared at her.

She nodded and hurried on. "Anyway, I met this guy
there my junior year. He was a senior and we dated all that
year. After he graduated, he took the summer off. He said
he'd have to work the rest of his life, and he wanted to enjoy himself—have one last fling. We saw each other almost
every day that summer." She shrugged. "I loved him and he
said he loved me. Now, of course, I realize we never talked
about the future, but then..." She trailed off, feeling so silly.
It was painful to admit you'd been a fool—if she'd been a
fool once, she could be one again.

"Anyway, I went back for my senior year and he got a job
on Wall Street and we saw each other maybe once a week,
but when we did, it was just as good as it had been." She
hesitated, then went on. "Just before Christmas, he invited
me to his home."

She looked around, seeing another house, deep in Fairfield County on Connecticut's Gold Coast. "His family had oodles of money, the kind that just sits in investment and trust funds and Swiss bank accounts, doubling and tripling in size." She sat down on a chaise and twisted her hands in her lap. "I thought he was going to ask me to marry him," she said quietly. "Instead, his mother announced his engagement to someone else. She told me I wasn't suitable— it seems my background was lacking, or something like that. So." She shrugged. "That was that."

Ryan stood with his hands shoved in his pockets, watching her. He nodded quietly. "Except it wasn't. It must have hurt you a great deal for you to be carrying around the pain years later."

She lifted sad eyes to Ryan. "Oh, Ryan," she said softly, "it wasn't just that." She looked around, as if the words she needed to explain herself might be lurking among the potted plants. "It was the realization that I'd been such a poor judge of character. I mean, I *loved* him. Yet that weekend, I saw him for what he was and..." She wrinkled her brow, recoiling from the memory. "I couldn't face it, Ryan. I couldn't face the fact that I'd loved this guy who was a perfect jerk. I couldn't face it that I'd been taken in by good looks and money and easy charm, or that I'd thought that I could fit into his world and was wrong. So I guess I rationalized it all away by telling myself that anyone who was rich was no good. They'd told me I wasn't good enough, after all, so I guess to save face, I turned it around and told myself they weren't."

Ryan sat down next to her. He clasped his hands and rested his arms on his thighs and nodded, looking at the floor. "I understand, Cass. I carried a lot of anger around with me for years." He reached out and took her hand and squeezed it. "But it's out now. Once you admit it and get it out, it can't harm you anymore."

She felt herself begin to smile, felt something lift inside her. "You're a very nice man, Ryan St. James," she said softly.

He leaned toward her and kissed her lingeringly. "And you're a very nice woman," he murmured. "What're we gonna do about it?"

She looked directly into his eyes and smiled. "I bet we'll think of something."

He nodded, giving her an answering smile. "Yeah," he whispered just before he kissed her again. "I bet we will...."

They made chowder together in Ryan's spacious kitchen, laughing and talking while listening to Ryan's old records. Ryan peeled and chopped the potatoes.

"You could call me the Potato King," he said, laughing. "I peeled more potatoes in the army than any other man on the face of the earth."

Cass laughed, removing the clams from the shells she'd steamed open and chopping them. The broth simmered on the stove, scenting the air with its briny tang and competing with the odor of the bacon sizzling in a frying pan. Outside, the rain continued, a steady downpour that made the kitchen seem even cozier.

"Making chowder reminds me of Cape Cod," she said dreamily. "When I was in college, a bunch of us worked summers on the Cape as waitresses. We rented a house and worked at night, then partied when we got off, slept until noon, and hit the beach all afternoon till we started work again at four." She smiled to herself. "Those were the days."

"I remember going to Galveston when I was a kid," Ryan said. "I'd never seen the ocean before. I was crazy about it.

I stood on the edge of the water and I remember thinking about who might be standing on the other side, in South America or Mexico, or even Europe. It blew my mind. Years later, when I'd made a lot of money and moved from Texas, I went to every beach I could visit—Florida and Atlantic City and Long Island, Cape Cod and Maine, Monaco, the south of France, the Greek Islands." He popped a clam into his mouth and washed it down with a swig of beer. "But, you know, I don't think I've ever tasted seafood like they make in Massachusetts and Rhode Island—Ipswich clams in Massachusetts and bay scallops off the Cape, and clam cakes in Rhode Island."

"Shore dinners," Cass said, rolling her eyes. "Dad used to take me once a year to Crescent Park in Rhode Island and we'd sit in a big old dining room, filled with wooden tables, and have lobster and steamers and corn on the cob, all *kinds* of food. The plates just *sagged* under it."

Ryan watched her with warm eyes. "Cass, I want to do all those things with you. I want to go to the Cape and Gloucester and Maine. I want to bring you to—what'd you say that place was you went with your dad?"

"Crescent Park."

"Yeah, there. And Coney Island. Jones Beach. Have you been to Atlantic City?"

She shook her head.

"Oh, Cass, you're gonna love it. It's not the gambling, it's the atmosphere. All those people, all kinds, Cass—old ones and young ones and everyone in between. Little old blue-haired ladies working the slots, and dapper guys with thin moustaches playing blackjack, and suburban couples blowing a couple hundred on dice, then going to the shows...." He trailed off. "Do you want to do those things with me, Cass?"

"I think I'd like to do almost anything with you, Ryan," she said softly.

He looked into her eyes, then his gaze roamed her face. "Cass, that rich guy was a loser, in more ways than one. Any man worth his salt wouldn't let you go once he got you." His voice lowered. "I know I don't intend to."

"Who sez you got me?" she asked laughingly, her green eyes sparkling.

Ryan pulled her into his arms. "You think I don't?" he asked, nuzzling her neck.

She took an unsteady breath, delighting in the butterflies that invaded her stomach. She ran her hands up his muscled chest and linked them behind his neck. "Do you?" she whispered.

His lips toyed with hers, brushing against them only to lift away tantalizingly. "I don't know," he murmured, teasing her with light kisses. "Let's see here . . ."

"Hey, what about supper?" she asked breathlessly. The chowder was ready to be heated; they just had to put it on the stove.

"Supper?" Ryan said, reluctantly letting go of her. "It's not supper I want right now, Cass," he said, shaking his head, his eyes suddenly dark.

She stared at him, feeling her heart begin to pound in her breast. Tonight, she realized—it would happen tonight. She couldn't stop it, didn't even want to try.

After dinner, Ryan built a fire and they sat in front of the hearth sipping wine. When they finished the bottle, he took her in his arms. "This is what I've wanted all day," he murmured, looking into her eyes. "You, in my arms, where you belong."

"It's what I've wanted, too," she whispered, trembling.

He groaned and tightened his arms around her, finding her lips hungrily. "You taste so good, Cass," he said between kisses. "You taste of wine and smell like roses. God, I want you so much."

"Oh, Ryan..." Her breath shook in her lungs. She ran her hands down his powerful chest, memorizing the planes and slopes of the muscles, coming to a stop at the second shirt button down. She toyed with it, hesitating, then made her decision. She wanted him as much as he wanted her. It was useless to deny it any longer.

Unbuttoning the second and third buttons on his shirt, she slid her hands inside, reveling at the contact with his warm skin. "You feel so good," she whispered.

"You have me at a disadvantage," he murmured huskily. "But if I unbutton your blouse, Cass, I'm not going to stop."

She lifted her eyes, knowing they were dark with desire. "I wouldn't want you to," she whispered.

He groaned and lifted her in his arms and carried her through the house to his room, then laid her carefully across his bed. He put his hands on either side of her head on the bed and leaned over her, staring down into her eyes. "You're sure, Cass?"

"Positive," she whispered, sliding her arms around his neck and pulling his head toward hers. "I know what I want."

His lips took hers in a honeyed kiss, stealing the breath from her body. She sank back against the pillows, feeling delicious tremors shake her as he unbuttoned her blouse and unhooked her bra. His hands were knowledgeable, coaxing her to respond. She tightened her arms around him, feeling a glorious surge of desire as she ran her hands over his muscled back.

"You taste so sweet," he murmured, his lips blazing a fiery path from the hollow of her throat to the valley between her breasts and opening over her nipple to suck it into his mouth. He laved it with his tongue, washing her in gentle, ever-rising circles of desire.

She groaned, tightening her arms around him, her eyes pressed tightly shut, her mouth open slightly in ecstasy. "Oh, yes," she whispered. "Yes."

He circled her nipple with his tongue, and she felt it harden into insistent urgency, felt his teeth scrape along its length, felt everything within her rise up in glorious response. She pulled his shirt from his trousers and slid her hands underneath, glorying in the smooth skin of his back, feeling him shiver at her touch. Feverishly, she finished unbuttoning his shirt with trembling fingers. Suddenly they were breathless, holding each other, struggling to remove their clothes, lost in the heady rush of discovery.

"You're beautiful," he breathed when at last their clothes were gone and they lay naked in each other's arms. He traced his forefinger from the hollow of her throat, between her breasts, down the slim line of her taut midriff to her navel, then rested his open palm on her flat abdomen. Her skin quivered in response, growing hot beneath his seeking hand.

"So are you," she whispered shakily, her eyes dark with suppressed desire. "More than beautiful. Magnificent."

"Touch me," he urged.

She drew in her breath and closed her eyes, drifting her hand down his lean body, glorying in the swell of hard muscles beneath his heated skin. At last she found him, and circled him gently with her fingertips, vibrantly aware that his breathing had quickened. He groaned and put his arms around her, seeking the soft swell of her buttocks with his hands, pulling her against him.

They lay together in exquisite torment, supremely aware of each other, of their mutual desire and need. "If I could have one thing on earth," Ryan whispered urgently, his dark eyes probing hers, "it would be to stay this way with you forever, just balanced on ecstasy the way we are now."

"Oh, Ryan." She kissed him feverishly, lost in the sweet, heady rush of rising passion. "It wouldn't last. It couldn't."

"It could," he insisted, returning her kisses with equal ardor. "I'd make it last. I'd never let it end." He kissed a fiery line down her throat to her breasts. "Never," he whispered as he touched his lips to her swollen nipple. "Never."

She sank into ecstasy, her body trembling, her eyes shut. He was a gentle lover at first, then when she was filled with so much need she cried out, his touch became equally insistent. She loved the hunger in his kisses, the need in his caresses, the way his breath shook and his eyes grew dark and his muscles bunched under her hands.

She felt as if a black, dark space had opened inside her, devouring her from within. Only one thing could save her, only one person could fill the void within her. "Please," she whispered. "Ryan, I need you."

He reached into his pants pocket to insure her protection, then turned back to her, gazing down at her lovingly. Then he eased inside her, increasing the power of his thrusts as he drove them into uncharted territory. She went with him, eyes squeezed shut in rapture, a sheen of sweat misting her body, hair lying in damp tendrils on her forehead. She followed him to a place of agony and abandon, finally exploding into beauty—a wave of light and soaring music.

Later, he lay on his side, smoothing his hand over the ripe curve of her hip, adoring her with his eyes. Her hair lay in glistening black waves around her shoulders, tumbling down her back. He lifted a strand and let it sift through his fingers.

"I have a fantasy," he said, his voice so low she could barely hear him.

"Do you?" she murmured.

He nodded, looking directly into her eyes. "You, leaning over me, with your hair forming a canopy around us, shutting out the world..."

She eased her leg over his. "Then what?" she whispered.

"Oh, Lord," he groaned. "What else?"

She sheathed him, then straddled his body. Her hair fell around them and they began to move together, eyes locked on each other as they rocked in a slow mating dance. He moved his hands down her naked back, traveling the planes and hollows to cup the rounded softness of her buttocks. He held her on him tightly, thrusting upward to meet her until at last they cried out in ecstasy and she collapsed onto his chest, breathing hard.

"So good," she murmured, her lips traveling over his chest to his neck. "So good..."

"Mmm." He ran his hand lovingly up her back to burrow under her hair. "Perfect." He kissed her deeply and put his arms around her, drawing her close. "Stay with me tonight, Cass. Sleep with me, and have breakfast with me, and read the paper with me. Don't ever leave, Cass."

How could a woman resist an invitation like that? She rolled onto her side and nestled against him, more contented than she'd ever been in her life. "You've got yourself a deal," she murmured sleepily.

Chuckling, Ryan drew the sheets over them and they slept.

Despite Ryan's position, he'd slept with few other women. One he'd loved to distraction, but had discovered belatedly she was only interested in the security his money could offer. The others he'd liked, but the liking hadn't turned to love. He lay in bed now and watched Cass, who lay sleeping on her stomach, her head turned toward him, her long hair lying around her like silken black netting.

What was it that attracted people to each other? he wondered. Why did most beautiful women leave him cold, and this beautiful woman heat his blood past all thought? He smiled to himself, realizing it wasn't her beauty that held him in thrall. That had probably been the initial attraction, but it wasn't the glue that held him. When he'd told her they were a lot alike, he hadn't been spouting a line designed to woo her; he'd meant it. He saw in Cass a lot of what he'd been, a lot of what he was now—a combination of guts, determination and sensitivity. He admired her spirit, but his heart melted at her vulnerability. He wanted to take her in his arms and protect her.

That was hopeless, of course. If he'd learned one thing, it was that everyone suffers his own torments and has to find his own way out. Some were lucky, and were able to negotiate the twists and turns in life and make their way into sunlight. But most weren't so lucky, and they stayed mired in unhappiness and anger, hating the world because they couldn't stand to face the role they play in their own unhappiness. Yesterday, when Cass had told him about her unhappy love affair, she'd stopped placing the blame on Geoff or the rich, and had finally taken responsibility for her own happiness.

Ryan rolled onto his back and stared at the ceiling. At least Cass had been more honest with him than he'd been with her. He was still hiding, still that frightened little kid in Texas, running from the truth. He bit off a groan and ran a tired hand over his face. If only it weren't so hard to talk about. If only he could be sure she'd understand.

Cass lay watching Ryan through her lashes. She'd never woken up with a man before. She and Geoff had always had to sneak time together, and she'd never stayed out with him all night; she'd been too worried about her dad's reaction.

Now she realized she liked not being furtive. All the time she'd been with Geoff she'd felt as if making love was shameful, but now she felt filled with joy, cleanly radiant, as if she'd been washed in light and bathed in beauty.

She frowned, watching as Ryan suppressed a sigh and rubbed his face tiredly. Her heartbeat quickened. For some reason, Ryan looked as if he felt guilty about something. She frowned at her mutinous thoughts, but wondered what could he feel guilty about. Ryan got out of bed and walked across to the wall of windows, then stood staring out. She lay in bed and watched him, seeing his naked body clearly for the first time. He was magnificent, all corded muscle and tough sinew, with broad shoulders and a strong back that tapered into a trim waist, small hips and tight buttocks. His thighs and calves were rock-hard with muscle and nicely covered with dark hair. She suppressed a shiver when she recalled the night before. Her body seemed made to be joined with his. That they would make love again was as certain as the course of the sun across the heavens, as inevitable as autumn following summer.

She sat up and called to him softly, "Ryan, is something wrong?"

He turned and the worry left his face as if by magic, replaced by a smile so radiant she knew instinctively that everything was all right. Whatever he'd been worried or guilty about had nothing to do with her. Mutely, she held out her hand, her lips softened with a smile, her green eyes filled with warmth.

Her breath caught in her throat. If he was magnificent from the back, he was doubly magnificent coming toward her. She felt her stomach curl deliciously within her; her breasts tingled with expectation. He was already aroused, his manhood clearly signalling his intent. She lay back, her hair splayed over the white sheets. Reaching up, she took his hand and placed it on her abdomen. She closed her eyes when she heard his low growl of pleasure. The bed shifted under his weight, then she felt the heat of his skin against hers.

It was like drinking water after wandering in the desert, yet they'd made love twice only hours before. Where had this incredible desire come from, this insatiable need? Her entire body seemed on fire with it, alive with hunger.

"Ryan," she whispered, "please. Now."

She heard his heavy breathing and knew he suffered from the same hunger, but he seemed to hesitate. She tightened her arms around him. "Ryan," she urged in a low voice that vibrated with desire, "please, I want you...."

He groaned, burying his face in her throat and twisting her hair in his fists. "In a minute," he whispered. "I don't have any protection...."

Startled from her desire, she lay back and watched him walk to his dresser and open the top drawer. She felt her ardor drain away. She had wanted him so much she hadn't been able to think, but even in the heat of passion, he'd kept his head. She turned on her side and pulled the sheet up, remembering that it had always been this way with Geoff. He'd always been frantic about birth control, and at first she'd been touched and had admired his sense of responsibility. It was only after she'd found out he didn't really love her that she'd realized why—he hadn't wanted to take even the slightest risk because he'd known their relationship was going nowhere. Cass knew that she should appreciate Ryan's concern, but somehow all she felt was a sense of profound rejection and she didn't look up when she felt the bed sag under Ryan's weight.

He put a gentle hand on her shoulder. "Cass?"

She refused to speak. She was embarrassed that she'd been so carried away when Ryan hadn't been. It was tantamount to admitting that she cared for him more than he cared for her. He was just like Geoff—he might sleep with her, but that momentary pleasure was the extent of his commitment. She wanted to press her face into the cool pillows and sob out her heartbreak, but she knew she had to pretend all was well.

Turning on her back, she looked up at him. "I'm sorry," she said. "I guess I got carried away. It wouldn't be too smart to get pregnant, would it?"

"Cass," he said softly, "let me explain."

"There's nothing to explain," she said cheerily, throwing back the sheet and bending to gather her clothes he'd thrown on the floor last night. "I understand," she said, dressing quickly. Now that the passion had subsided, she knew he'd been right to want to take precautions, but she was embarrassed that she'd wanted him so much she couldn't even think straight. She took refuge in teasing irony. "It wouldn't do for the great Ryan St. James to get caught in embarrassing circumstances, would it? That's all you'd need—some money-hungry woman bringing a paternity suit against you. The gossip columns would have a field day."

"Cass, damn it, listen to me!" He put his hands on her shoulders and turned her to face him. She fell silent, surprised at the anger in his face. "That's not what I'm worried about at all," he said. "You're not the kind of woman to do that, and anyway, if I got you pregnant, I'd marry you in a minute."

"I see," she said, trying to sound like she was joking. "So that's it. You just don't want to get trapped."

"That's right," he agreed, "I don't. What kind of way is that to start a marriage?"

She stared at him; what could she say? He was right, which only made her angry. She slipped out from under his hand. "I think it's time for me to go home, Ryan."

"Cass, let me explain...."

"I'll wait in the kitchen for you. You will drive me home, won't you?" She didn't wait for his answer, but turned and escaped from the room, unintentionally slamming the door behind her. The sound echoed in the silent corridor as she fled, anger and hurt warring within her.

Nine

Cass was halfway through the house when Ryan caught up with her. "Cass, are you running away from me?" he asked.

She faltered, then came to a stop. "No," she said, her back still to him. "Why should you think that?"

"Cass..." He put his hand on her arm and drew her back against him, nuzzling the side of her neck with his lips. "Honey, come back to bed with me."

She closed her eyes and tried not to shiver at the sensuality that slumbered in his low voice. It would have been so simple to turn into his arms and respond to his caresses, but she couldn't allow herself to. There was no future with Ryan St. James. She'd been a fool to even go out with him. She had to put a stop to this thing now, before she fell completely in love.

"I'm sorry, Ryan," she said, injecting coolness into her voice, "but I really do have to go. Will you take me, or shall I call my uncle to come get me?"

She waited for his answer stiffly, refusing to turn around and face him. She could feel his confusion and frustration, could hear his anger when he responded.

"Of course I'll take you home," he said, his voice clipped. He walked past her, pushing open the front door. "Well?" he said from the front step. "Are you coming?"

He was looking annoyed, she noticed as she passed him on the way to his car. His blue eyes glittered at her and a muscle jumped in his cheek. Before she knew it, they were in the car, the motor was roaring, and they were off in a flurry of gravel and exhaust smoke. "I really dislike it when men drive recklessly," she said. "That kind of behavior is always a cover for an ego the size of a pin."

"Better a small ego than—" he broke off abruptly, but let up on the accelerator.

"I suppose you were going to say something about me just then," Cass murmured, eyes straight ahead.

"I was," he said shortly, "but I thought better of it."

She turned her head and stared out the window, feeling sick inside. He had every right to be angry, she realized—she'd stalked out of his room without even telling him what she was so upset about, and yet she couldn't bring herself to talk with him. She was too vulnerable, too afraid she already cared more than he did.

Suddenly, Ryan downshifted, then coasted to a stop. "What's all this about, Cass? Do you mind letting me in on it?"

What could she say? That she was involved in a last-ditch attempt to salvage her badly mangled ego? There wasn't any excuse for her behavior. "Just take me home, Ryan," she said, dropping her gaze to her hands, which were clutched in her lap.

"No," Ryan said. "I'm not budging till we get to the bottom of this."

At last, she turned to look at him. "I just want to go home, Ryan," she said, her voice almost breaking.

Suddenly the anger left his face. "Cass," he said gently, "half an hour ago, you wanted to make love with me. It looks to me like you don't know what you want. Maybe if we sit here awhile, you'll decide you don't want to go home after all."

She lifted her chin. "I'm afraid I've made up my mind. I want to go home."

He studied her with narrowed eyes. "I think we need to talk."

"There's nothing to talk about, Ryan," she said tiredly. "You want one thing; I want another. Just take me home and let's chalk it all up to a pleasant weekend interlude."

"Is that all this was to you?" he asked sharply. "A romp in the hay?"

She stared at him, astonished to see that he appeared hurt. "That's how you view it, isn't it? Just another good time? A good-time guy out with a good-time girl."

"I'm not a good-time guy," he said. "And I sure as hell don't think of you as a good-time girl. I think I know what this is all about; you're angry about what happened this morning. But what would've happened if we'd made love and I'd gotten you pregnant?"

That was the issue, she realized. Ryan wanted her today, but he might not a couple of weeks from now. After a couple weeks of rest and recreation, he'd be ready to return to New York and set the world on fire. There wouldn't be any room in his life for a woman from the wrong side of the tracks. As difficult as it was to admit, she was thankful he'd used his head. It was going to be hard enough to forget Ryan St. James; she certainly didn't need the complication of getting pregnant in the bargain.

"You're right, Ryan," she said quietly. "I wasn't thinking straight."

He fingered a strand of her hair. "I'm glad you understand, Cass."

She turned her head and stared bleakly out the window. He couldn't have made his feelings more clear if he'd stood on the Empire State Building and shouted them to the world. Ryan St. James didn't want to get involved in a serious relationship. He'd taken a few weeks off from work and wanted to play. He also wanted to make sure she knew that's all it would be. But Cass felt more for Ryan than gratitude for a weekend romp. She couldn't spend any more time with him, knowing it would end and he'd walk out of her life. She threw him a light smile and shook back her hair. "I think you'd better take me home now, Ryan. I have a lot of things to do before I go back to work tomorrow."

"But I don't want to take you home," he protested. "I want to spend the day with you. Hell, I want to spend the rest of the weekend with you."

"I don't think that's a very good idea," she said carefully. "I'm not ready for a relationship right now."

"Then what was yesterday and last night?"

She stared at him. If she didn't know he didn't want to get involved, she'd almost swear he was hurt. "Chalk it up to summer romance," she said lightly. "And active, healthy hormones, on both our parts."

"It wasn't just hormones, Cass," he said, his blue eyes suddenly dark. "I know what 'just sex' feels like. This was different."

She looked away, suddenly afraid. If he talked her into returning to his house with him, she'd be lost. There was no way she could keep herself from falling in love with him. At twenty-six, she was too old to let herself get involved in another one-way love affair. She'd nursed a broken heart too long to let Ryan trample all over it now.

"I'm sorry, Ryan," she said quietly. "But I'd really rather not get involved with you."

"Damn it," he said, sounding more than a little exasperated, "you already *are* involved with me, Cass."

"No, Ryan," she said. "If I went back to your house with you right now, I would be, but I'm not now. Take me home, please."

He stared at her, a muscle working agitatedly in his cheek. "For the first time in my life, I'm tempted to ignore my gentlemanly instincts and turn this car around and take you back to bed and keep you there till you come to your senses."

Cass felt her mouth go dry. An insidious longing crept through her and for a moment she wished he'd do just that, then she rallied. She couldn't let her heart rule her mind—the stakes were too high. "Take me home, Ryan," she said coolly. "I really have a lot of work to do." Tense with expectation and anxiety, she waited, then felt a strange regret mingled with relief as he put the car into gear and eased it onto the road.

At her house, he placed a hand on her arm before she got out of the car. "This isn't the last you'll see me, Cass. I'm not giving up."

She looked down at the hand on her arm and was both exhilarated and frightened. "Don't bother to call, Ryan. I'm not interested."

He looked at her as if he didn't believe her, then pulled her into his arms and kissed her. For just a moment, she tried to fight him, then her body betrayed her. Her arms crept around his neck, and her mouth opened under his probing tongue. "*Now* tell me you're not interested," he murmured when the kiss ended.

She put her palms against his chest as if to ward off his potent male attraction. "We're good in bed, Ryan," she said. "But that's all."

"How do you know?" he asked roughly. "You haven't even given us a chance."

"We don't have a chance," she said, opening the door and getting out. "You want one thing and I want something else entirely. Goodbye, Ryan." She closed the car door and raced toward the house.

When Cass pulled into Chick-O-Rama's parking lot the next day, Ryan's car was there. She felt a momentary lifting of her spirits, then came to her senses. He was probably here to ask her out, but she wasn't interested in a two-week affair. If she had to, she'd manufacture anger. The sooner he left, the better off she'd be.

He was seated on a stool at the minuscule counter, munching on a piece of fried chicken, talking with her uncle. Cass slammed the door shut. "What are you doing here?" she demanded.

"Hey!" Uncle Henry said, looking astounded. "Is that any way to talk to a customer?"

"He's not a customer, Henry," Cass said.

"Afternoon, Cass," Ryan said affably.

"You two know each other?" Henry asked, looking from one to the other.

They answered at the same time; she said no and he said yes.

Choosing to ignore him, she sailed past him on her way to the kitchen. "You can go now, Henry. I'll put the next batch of chicken on."

"Go?" Henry said, eyes gleaming. He followed her into the kitchen. "Do you think I'm gonna leave what promises to be the best story I've seen since 'Peyton Place' went off the air?''

"There's no *story*, as you put it," Cass said huffily, then asked under her breath, "How long has he been here?"

"Ryan?" Henry mused, scratching his chin. He turned and shouted back to the front, "How long you been here, Ryan? A couple hours?"

Cass groaned. It was worse than she could have expected. Ryan had gained Henry's confidence and they were already on a first name basis. "He's just here to bother me, Henry," she said, tying on an apron and beginning to take chicken parts from the refrigerator.

"No, he isn't," Henry said, sounding pleased as punch. "We've been talking business."

Cass froze. Slowly, she turned to face Uncle Henry. Ryan appeared in the doorway behind him. "You *what*?"

"We've been talking business, Cass," Henry said. "Course I told Ryan I wouldn't make any decision without consulting you first, you being my partner and all."

"Decision..." She stared in horror at her uncle, then looked at Ryan. He hadn't been interested in her in the least, and she'd been too foolish to see it! The full realization of what he'd been doing hit her, and her green eyes sizzled.

"How dare you!" she said in a low voice. "You come in here with all your money and your business reputation and talk to an old man about selling out and he falls for it!"

"Now just a darn minute, Cass," Uncle Henry said. "Who are you calling an old man?"

"We're not selling," Cass said to Ryan, ignoring her uncle. "Is that clear? We're not interested."

"Selling?" Looking puzzled, Henry looked from Cass to Ryan. "What are you talking about?"

"Oh, Henry," she said, putting a hand on his arm. "I didn't mean to say you were old. It's just..." She looked back at Ryan, anger and disillusionment glittering in her eyes. "You're too trusting, Henry. You'd trust the local bookie with your life. You've got to realize when someone as big as Ryan St. James wants to shut us down—"

"Shut us down?" Henry stared at her as if she were certifiable. "What in Sam Hill are you talking about, Cass? Ryan's been talking business with me. He likes my chicken."

"Well of course he likes it!" Cass said, laughing shortly. "Anyone with half a mind would. You make the best chicken in Waterbury."

"Then why's Chick-O-Rama in the red, Cass?" Ryan asked quietly.

It was the first time he'd spoken. He was leaning against the wall, his arms folded across his powerful chest. He wore a pair of khaki pants and a white polo shirt and looked good enough to have for lunch. Cass forced that kind of treacherous thought out of her mind and concentrated instead on his duplicity.

"Who says we are?" she asked defiantly. She glanced at her uncle, her heart sinking. If Ryan St. James came in here and wormed a lot of financial secrets out of Henry, she'd deck her uncle!

"Oh, Cass," Henry said, gesturing around them. "It doesn't take too much to see we aren't exactly flourishing here."

"And I suppose *he* says he wants to help," she sneered, nodding at Ryan. "All out of the goodness of his heart of gold."

"As a matter of fact—"

"Henry," Ryan interrupted. "Can I speak with you alone a minute?"

Henry looked from Ryan to Cass, then shrugged. "Sure."

"Uncle Henry, don't listen to him! The man is a shark. He senses blood in the water and he's circling."

Ryan slowly uncrossed his arms, his face unreadable. He pushed away from the wall and left the kitchen with Uncle Henry, throwing a final look at Cass that made her writhe. She turned her back and chewed on her thumbnail. Something about the way Ryan had looked at her filled her with shame. But *he* was the one sneaking around behind her back, trying to buy the business! She had no intention of apologizing for what she'd said. Ryan was the one who needed to apologize—he'd taken her out and wined and dined her, had even slept with her, when all along he wanted only one thing—to buy out Chick-O-Rama.

When was she ever going to learn to judge men? She'd been taken in by Geoff Sutton and she'd almost been taken in by Ryan St. James. Was she such a mental lightweight that every good-looking man who came along fooled her so easily? She closed her eyes and sank into a chair, unable to fight the pain that went through her like a lance. Yesterday, she'd held out a slim hope that she'd been wrong about Ryan. Now she knew she wasn't, and she was amazed at the pain that realization cost her.

She looked up when Henry appeared in the doorway. "Ryan left. He said to say goodbye."

"He left? Just like that?"

Henry nodded, eyeing her curiously. "Why didn't you tell me you knew him?"

"Because I don't know him that well."

"That's not how I hear it."

Cass's face blazed. "Henry, it's none of your business."

"No, but this place is," he snapped. Then he groaned and sat down opposite her. "I'm sorry, Cassie. It's just you get me so mad sometimes. Why didn't you talk to me about what happened between you and Ryan St. James?"

"Because nothing happened," she said shortly, standing up.

Henry reached out and took her hand and forced her gently back into the chair. "Cass," he said tiredly. "Ryan didn't make any offer to buy the business."

She stared at her uncle, confused. "He didn't?"

"No. He came in here and ordered some chicken and we got to talkin' and first thing you know, he tells me who he is and we talked about running businesses and one thing led to another and he gave me some advice—good advice."

"Henry," she said softly, her green eyes filled with sadness. "Don't you see? Ryan St. James didn't just come in here to have some chicken. He came in here for a purpose. The first day I met him, he pulled out his checkbook and offered to buy us out. I could've named the price."

"We talked about that just now, Cass. He admits he made a mistake."

"Of course he admits it!" she said, squeezing her uncle's hands. "Don't you see, Henry? That method didn't work, so now he's going to try another."

Henry looked at her, his watery blue eyes filled with sorrow, then he shook his head. "You're the one doesn't understand, Cass," he said finally. "Ryan warned me you wouldn't."

"And you're taking his side, aren't you?" She sat back, stung at the way her uncle had turned against her. When a smooth talker like Ryan St. James came around, he could turn family against family. The thought of having that much power frightened her.

"Cass, I'm not takin' sides! Ryan isn't out to get us."

"Henry, just promise me one thing. Don't think about selling yet. I think we can get back on top of things again. We'll need to go to a bank and talk about a loan, but I think we can do it."

Henry seemed about to say something, then stopped himself. "Cass, why in tarnation would Ryan St. James want to buy our business? Hell, he's so rich he could start up fifty chicken restaurants if he wanted to."

"Who knows why a man like Ryan wants anything?" Cass said. "Maybe he *doesn't* want the business! Not to run it anyway. He thinks it's ugly—he called it an eyesore. Maybe it's just a point of pride with him, Henry. He made an offer and he won't be happy until he gets what he wants." She shook her head, eyes blazing. "I don't have any idea why he wants it, Henry. All I know is, there is just no way Ryan St. James is going to get this business. I mean it, Henry. We've got to hold on."

Henry scratched his chin, then shrugged. "I don't know, Cass. I'm gettin' old and have even been thinkin' of retiring, but if you're keen on making a go of this place, I suppose it wouldn't hurt to talk to a banker...."

"That's the spirit!" She threw her arms around him and kissed him soundly. "Talk to one today, Henry. Ryan'll be livid when he finds out we're not going to sell."

Amusement glittered in Henry's eyes and he began to chuckle.

"What are you laughing about?" Cass asked suspiciously.

"Who's laughin'?" Henry asked, wiping the smile off his face and looking misunderstood. He placed a meaty hand on his heart. "Me? Laugh?"

Cass eyed him speculatively. If she didn't know better, she'd think he was up to something.

Ten

Thursday, Cass stood in the doorway of Chick-O-Rama, staring balefully across the street at Burger City. A steady stream of cars drove up, stopped, and emptied their cargo. As families, couples and lone customers all streamed into Burger City, Cass could almost hear the cash registers clicking. She glanced at the clock and wondered where Uncle Henry was. He was supposed to find out if they'd gotten the loan from the bank. She didn't like it that Henry controlled all the finances of the business, but her inherited portion was only forty percent. When Uncle Henry first started out, he'd run Chick-O-Rama alone, and he'd remained the senior partner even when his younger brother had joined him. The trouble was, Henry wasn't a financial wizard—the state of Chick-O-Rama was testimony to that.

Cass walked back to the cramped office and stared down at the column of figures. She'd spent the past two days drawing up a plan. First, they'd spruce up Chick-O-Rama a bit. They'd paint the outside, landscape, and redo the interior. The menu would stay the same—chicken was their product, and they were going to go with it. But the name Chick-O-Rama...

Cass frowned. She'd been pushing Henry to change the name for ages and had spent the better part of a day trying to come up with a new one. She just couldn't decide on one. Henry had been adamant.

"The name is Chick-O-Rama!" he'd said. "It started out that way and it'll end that way!"

"If we keep the name, it *will* end, Henry," Cass had warned. "If we're going to renovate, we should get a new name, too. Something to let people know we're changing."

"But we're not changing!" Henry had yelled. "The chicken'll stay the same!"

"That's the only thing that *will* be the same, Henry." She'd shaken her head, puzzled over not being able to come up with the right name. "That's all right, it'll come to me."

But here she was, still stymied, and she'd already hired a sign painter, only he couldn't start on a new sign until she gave him the new name. She wanted to take a huge ad out in the paper, but she couldn't very well do that if they were changing the name. "Chicken Deluxe," she said out loud. "Top Chick. Big Chick." She rolled her eyes and slumped in the ancient oak chair, staring up at the cracked ceiling. "Henry's Chicken. Uncle Henry's Chicken..." She sighed and sat up. It was no use. The name wouldn't come to her.

Then the door burst open and Henry ran in. "We got it!"

Cass catapulted out of her chair and threw her arms around him. "We did? Oh, Henry, I'm so happy!"

"I've been thinkin', Cass."

She tilted her head. "Oh?"

"Yeah." He spread his hands out as if envisioning something. "If we have to change the name, how 'bout calling it Dickens' Chickens?"

"Uh . . . well, it's different. . . ."

"You don't like it."

"I didn't say that."

"Huh." He shrugged out of his rumpled suit coat. "Have you come up with a better name?"

She shook her head. "It's no use. The more I think, the worse they get."

"You'll come up with one, Cassie."

She looked up, surprised. "I thought you wanted to keep Chick-O-Rama."

"I do." He shrugged. "But you're so set on changing it, I decided I wouldn't fight it."

Cass put her arms around his considerable middle and rested her cheek against his shoulder. "All bark and no bite, Henry. That's you."

He patted her shoulder and chuckled, then frowned. "I dunno though, Cass. I kinda like Dickens' Chickens. . . ."

"Henry," she groaned. "You cook the stuff. I'll name it."

"Better name it soon," Henry warned. "We can't put that ad in the paper if we don't have a new name."

She nodded, her forehead creased in thought. "Something just came to me."

"Yeah?" Henry waited. "Well?"

"Chickenland," she said slowly. "Come on over to Chickenland, home of the best fried chicken you ever tasted." She looked at Henry. "How does that sound?"

His gaze fell from hers as he shrugged. "Not bad."

"If Walt Disney could start Disneyland, why can't we start Chickenland?"

Henry lifted his eyebrows and pursed his lips. "Well, I guess we could..."

She watched his expressive face and knew he hated the name. He couldn't hide his feelings from her if he put a bag over his head. "I'll think a little more about it, Uncle Henry," she said slowly, then roused herself. "I suppose if I really wanted to get back at Ryan St. James, I'd just leave the name alone."

Henry's face took on a thoughtful look. "You think about him a lot, don't you, Cass?"

"Who?" As if she didn't know.

"Ryan."

She shrugged. "No more than I have to," she said, and turned and walked out.

"Cassie?"

"Yeah?" She turned to look back at her uncle. He stuck his head around the door and smiled at her.

"You never could lie convincingly. Not even when you were a kid."

She made a face at him. "I don't want to talk about him, understand?"

"Who's talkin' about him?" he asked, sounding hurt.

Cass watched him tie an apron on and shuffle into the kitchen, muttering the entire time.

Cass's smile faded quickly. Turning, she glanced across the street at Burger City. She should be happy, she realized. She should be jumping with joy. She and Uncle Henry had gotten a loan and they'd soon be refurbishing Chick-O-Rama, yet she didn't feel like celebrating. Instead, she had the most absurd desire to be with Ryan again, even if it were just for two short weeks.

She was halfway home late that afternoon when she realized Ryan was following her. She took a couple turns, hoping to shake him off, but was unsuccessful. When she drove into her driveway, her heart was thumping madly as she wondered what he would pull now. Would he try to convince her he wanted to go out with her, or would he simply make another offer on the business? She felt anger bubble up inside her, but vowed to control it.

"Slumming, Mr. St. James?" she asked airily as she walked past him to the front door.

"No, Ms. Dickens," he said, falling into step beside her. "Just here for a friendly chat."

She turned on him, her green eyes flashing. "No," she said. "I'm not interested in anything you have to say—period."

"You're jumping to conclusions, Cass."

She opened the door and stepped onto the screened porch. "Goodbye, Mr. St. James," she said, closing the door firmly. "I'm afraid I can't say it was a pleasure knowing you."

She turned to go, but he said, "Cass, you're wrong. I didn't offer to buy your business when I talked with Henry."

She hesitated, then shook herself and walked to the front door. For some reason, the key wouldn't fit in the lock, then she realized her fingers were shaking. She heard the screen door open, heard Ryan's footsteps, then there was only silence.

"I went there to see you," he said from just behind her. "Henry and I got to talking. I realized pretty fast that you hadn't told him about going out with me, so I didn't tell him I was there to see you."

She stared down at the doorknob, where the key was not quite in the lock. She should open the door and get in the house as fast as she could. She shouldn't stand here with Ryan so near, and listen to him.

"We did talk about business, Cass, but I only made a couple of suggestions."

She nodded curtly. "Sure—like sell you our business."

"No," Ryan said, sounding angry. "I told Henry what I did when I was in his shoes—I got a loan."

Cass turned around slowly. Ryan just stood and stared at her, his lips set in a thin line, his eyes crackling with suppressed anger. "I told him he made the best damned chicken I've ever tasted, and said he'd be foolish not to put some money into the business and develop it. I also told him that he needed a business plan. Lots of people go out of business because they simply lack business sense, not because their products aren't any good." He nodded curtly. "Okay, that's all I came for."

He turned to leave, but Cass called out. "Don't go." He paused, but he didn't turn back. She reached out and put a hand on his arm. "Please, Ryan."

He looked back at her, his eyes angry. "Why the hell should I stay?" he asked. "You wouldn't even give me the benefit of the doubt." He shook his head. "Maybe you're right. Maybe we do want completely different things."

She stared at him, so frightened she was shaking. She had to take a chance. If she didn't, she might kick herself forever. "I want a man who wants me for more than two weeks, Ryan. I won't just go to bed with you knowing in a couple of weeks you'll leave and never look back."

He tilted his head consideringly. "Is that what you think? That I just want you now and when I go back to New York, I'll never call?"

She looked away. His eyes were too blue, too filled with questions. "You made it abundantly clear that you don't want to get trapped in any way." She frowned. "I don't know how to say it, Ryan, but somehow you communicated some kind of..." She hesitated, searching for the word she needed. "Well, some kind of fear, almost. The thought of my getting pregnant seemed repugnant to you, as if the idea of any kind of commitment was intolerable." She looked back at him, meeting his eyes directly. "I mean, if I *cared* for the man..." She faltered. She'd said too much. It was time to stop talking.

"Go on," he said gently. "If you cared for the man...?"

She shrugged. "I guess you're just one of those men who doesn't want to get involved in a relationship." She looked up and met his eyes. "But I do, Ryan. I want a home and kids and a husband who cares about us all. So, you see, we both just want different things. I'm not the woman for you."

"You *are* the woman for me," he said, so softly she wasn't certain she heard him correctly. But then he took her in his arms and she knew she must have. "I want you," he said as he kissed her face. "I'm not afraid of getting involved, Cass, but I can't figure out how we could get involved if we don't see more of each other."

She felt a sweet tide of emotion wash over her and wrapped her arms around his neck. "Do you mean it?" she whispered against his lips.

"Yes," he breathed. "I mean it more than you'll ever know."

She shivered. His voice was low and his breath feathered across her lips. She went up on tiptoe and ran a hand into the dark thickness of his hair. "Oh, Ryan," she whispered.

"Sweet Cass," he murmured, kissing her lazily, as if feeding on the sweetness of her lips. He ran his hands up and down her back, then pulled her hips close to his. "Lord," he growled into the side of her neck. "I want you so bad I'm on fire."

She closed her eyes and clung to him. "Me too."

"Oh, Cass," he said, pressing kisses along her neck and nuzzling her earlobe. "If I told you what I want to do with you right now, you'd be shocked. You'd wonder how a man could appear so civilized and be such an animal underneath."

She shivered again and splayed her hands over his back. "Then why don't you just show me?" she whispered.

He groaned and searched for the key in her hands, then somehow unlocked and opened the door. "Come on," he said, sweeping her into his arms and shutting the door with his foot. "Where's the nearest bed?"

Between kisses, she directed him to her bedroom, but they didn't get very far. He stopped in the hall and kissed her deeply, still holding her in his arms. She wrapped her arms around his neck and kissed him back wholeheartedly and when the kiss ended, Ryan leaned against the wall, as if weak. "Ever want somebody so bad your knees buckle?" he asked.

She nodded, nuzzling his neck with her nose. "Mm hm. I've felt that way with you."

He put her down, but kept her body pressed intimately into his. "Can't get to a bed, Cass," he murmured between kisses. "Want you right here." He combed her hair around her shoulders, then balled it in his fists and groaned. "I never knew it could be like this—so sweet—so much hunger....I want you more than I've ever wanted anything in my life," he murmured as he caressed her back and hips.

She took his hand and led him down the hall into her bedroom. She stood in front of him and began unbuttoning her blouse. When he reached out for her, she backed away, shaking her head.

"No," she whispered. "Just watch."

He sat on the edge of the bed as she unfastened her blouse and dropped it to the floor, then stepped out of her slacks. She walked slowly forward, her long hair falling around her shoulders in abundant ebony waves. She came to a stop just in front of him and took off her bra and stepped out of her panties.

Ryan's control broke. He gathered her to him, pressing his face into her stomach, his hands cupping her buttocks, lazily caressing her satin skin with his lips and tongue. She caught her breath, then ran her hands into his hair, gasping as his tongue traced an erotic pathway down her abdomen. What had begun for her as a pleasant sensual game became a dire necessity. She tore open the buttons of his shirt and moaned when she came in contact with the smooth, sweet texture of his skin.

He slid his hand into the juncture of her legs and she gasped, arching her back and pressing against him as he massaged her with knowing fingers. Frenzied now, they tumbled onto the bed. He gathered her into his warm embrace, his lips scorching her skin, finding each intimate spot and claiming it as his own. She grew dizzy with passion, overwhelmed by a need that seemed cataclysmic. Her desire mounted, even when he stopped to sheathe himself.

It was a passionate joining, all elemental hunger, raw and primitive. She felt as if she encompassed him, that she could open and flower and take him so deeply inside he might become part of her forever. It seemed the object of her body, for she locked her knees around his back, and met him thrust for thrust. The world receded until only they remained, locked in loving combat, bodies joined so deeply they were one.

They hung in rapture on the edge of fulfillment, then Ryan thrust deeply into her and their world splintered with glory. Gradually, they descended from the Olympian height, and lay wrapped in each other's arms.

When the last fingers of light crept out of the room, Cass lay on her side, looking into his eyes as he combed strands of her dark hair with his fingers. "Do you think it's this way for everyone?" she asked.

He smiled and shook his head. "No. What we have is special."

"I think you're right," she whispered, nestling against his chest.

He ran his hand down her back and rested it on the fullness of her hip. "I suppose we should think about eating supper."

"Are you hungry?"

"I'm getting there," he said, grinning, then rubbed his chin against her shoulder. "Should I shave?"

"In the morning," she whispered.

"You mean you'll let me stay the night?" he teased.

She raised herself up on one elbow. "If you tried to leave," she said, rubbing her nose against his, "I'd tie you up and keep you here."

"How long?"

"Forever."

"Then I'm trying to leave."

She laughed softly and buried her head in his shoulder. "I'm so glad you came after me, Ryan."

"So'm I," he murmured, running his hand up and down her back. "You tried my patience severely, Ms. Dickens, but this was worth it."

She suddenly grew serious. "Ryan, I'm sorry about the way I doubted you. Uncle Henry tried to tell me it was ridiculous that you'd want Chick-O-Rama, but I wouldn't listen. I kept remembering the first day we met, when you took one look at it and whipped out that fat checkbook of yours."

He groaned and rolled onto his back. "Yeah," he said, rubbing his eyes tiredly. "That was pretty stupid."

"Why did you do it?" Cass asked, sitting up and searching for her robe.

He rubbed his chin thoughtfully. "It's hard to explain, Cass. You were looking at me with all that fire in your eyes and I was attracted to you immediately. I like a good fight, Cass—always have, probably always will. I wanted to see how far you'd go to defend your turf."

"What if I'd said yes? What if I'd said I'd sell Chick-O-Rama? Would you have bought it?"

He chuckled and pulled her into his arms. "Now why on earth would I want a crummy old chicken restaurant?"

For no reason, she shivered, wondering momentarily if perhaps that wasn't exactly what he wanted, then she tried to hide her reaction by pretending to be angry. "Crummy old...!" She managed to evade his kisses, fending him off. "I'll have you know Uncle Henry and I got a loan today."

"Oh?"

Did he appear more interested than she expected? Cass frowned, then shook off her doubts. "We did. We're going to spruce up the place and do a little advertising."

"That's great, Cass. Your uncle's chicken is the best I've ever tasted, and that's coming from a man whose mother is a great Southern cook."

"You really think it's good?"

"It's great." He chuckled and sat up, reaching for his trousers. "Hell, it's better than my Chicken Chunx any day."

"You admit it?" she cried, eyes glowing. "You really mean it?"

"Yeah, I really mean it." He grinned at her. "And speaking of food, I've got an appetite that would do justice to a barracks full of Marines." He pulled her into his arms and nibbled on her shoulder. "But I guess I could make do with this...."

Laughing, Cass wrapped her arms around him. "I don't have a thing in the house to eat. We can go out for dinner or I could scrounge up some bread and make French toast."

Ryan searched her eyes. "Which would you prefer, Cass? Would you like to go out? We could find some candlelit, four-star restaurant that would treat you like a queen, if you want."

She hesitated, then shook her head. "Crazy as it sounds, I'd just like to stay here with you. If you don't mind, that is."

"I don't mind." He drew her into his arms and his eyes grew serious. "Funny thing is, anything with you sounds just fine. French toast or filet mignon, just as long as I'm with you."

Cass closed her eyes and sank into his arms. For the next two weeks, she wasn't going to think. She was just going to follow the logic of her heart.

Eleven

"Tell me about your Uncle Henry," Ryan said.

They were seated at her kitchen table the following morning. The breakfast plates were scraped clean of the maple syrup and butter that had oozed off the French toast Cass had prepared. Steam rose lazily from the coffee in their cups. On the radio, a pianist played a Chopin étude. Puss slumbered in a puddle of sun on a braided rug, twitching and growling, as if pursuing field mice in his dreams.

"Uncle Henry," Cass mused, smiling. "He's wonderful, but I'd never admit it to his face. He and Dad ran Chick-O-Rama for thirty-four years. After Dad died and left me his share of the business, I decided I might as well get involved."

"What'd you do before you started at Chick-O-Rama?"

"I was produce manager at a grocery store," she said. "It wasn't the most exciting work in the world, but it paid the bills."

"I thought you said you went to Yale. How'd you end up in a supermarket?"

"I dropped out of Yale," she said shortly, standing up to clear the table. "More coffee?"

"Dropped out?" He shook his head and put a hand over his cup when she held out the coffee. "Why'd you do that?"

"You're worse than Uncle Henry!" she said, grinning. "I just decided I wasn't college material, that's all."

"But you said you met your old boyfriend when you were a junior at Yale, so you had to have been almost finished when you dropped out."

"I was a senior," she said, beginning to run water into the dishpan. "You want to wash or dry?"

"Dry." He took the dish towel she held out. "Why'd you drop out?"

Cass groaned, throwing him an exasperated look. "What's it matter? It's ancient history now, water over the dam." She shoved a glass at him. "Here. Dry."

He took the glass and dried it thoughtfully, then held it up to the light, squinting at it with one eye closed. "You were a senior at one of the most prestigious universities in the country, and you dropped out." He snapped his fingers. "Just like that."

She looked at him, nodding. "Yeah." She snapped her fingers, too. "Just like that."

He looked at her seriously. "It was that Geoff guy, wasn't it? He not only messed up your heart, he messed up your head."

She looked at the fluffy bubbles that floated in the red rubber dishpan, not sure she wanted to talk about it. Still, if she and Ryan were ever going to get to know each other, she'd have to learn to share her fears and feelings with him— both past and present. The only problem was, that meant facing her feelings herself, and coming to grips with them and everything they represented.

"I was devastated after what happened with Geoff," she said slowly. "I ended up flunking a course that semester, which meant I wouldn't be able to graduate on time anyway. After semester break, I just never went back."

"So why not go back now?"

"Because now I haven't got the full scholarship I did then."

"Take out a loan," he said. "Other people do. It'd only be for a year."

She frowned thoughtfully. "It's hard to explain, Ryan, but when Geoff and his family told me I wasn't good enough, I was so angry I decided I didn't want to change myself or anything about my life. Not going back to Yale was like making a statement. It was as if I were saying, 'I *am* good enough, just the way I am.'"

"Fine. You know it and I know it, so you've made your point. Go back and get your degree, Cass. Stop cutting off your nose to spite your face."

She handed him a plate. "Sorry," she said lightly, "but I have a job now. I've got a two-bit chicken restaurant to pull out of the financial doldrums." She grinned at him. "Trouble is, there's a glitzy new burger joint across the street that's cutting into my business." She made a face at him. "And that wouldn't be so bad, but they're selling some kind of processed cardboard they call Chicken Chunx."

"Cardboard!" he echoed, grinning back. "They're made from one hundred percent chicken parts."

"Chicken parts," Cass said knowingly. "Yeah, like beaks and feet."

"Have you ever tried them?"

"Are you kidding?" she crowed. "I had some of those nugget things at one of your competitors one time and once was enough." She shook her head. "Nope, I eat the real thing, brother, or nothin' at all."

"Okay, that's it." He put the dish towel down and untied her apron. "I know where we're going for lunch."

"Lunch!" she protested, laughing as he pulled her in his wake through the house. "We just had breakfast."

He put an arm playfully around her and pulled her against him. "Gotta fatten you up, Cass," he said, kissing her soundly. "I like my women Rubenesque...."

Chicken Chunx, it turned out, were oval pieces of processed chicken, breaded and deep-fried, and served in a cardboard container shaped like a henhouse. Cass's eyes danced as she sat in the air-conditioned comfort of Burger City and watched Ryan walk back to the table carrying two ridiculous cardboard henhouses.

"Clever," she said, nodding at them when he set them on the table.

"The marketing director's idea," Ryan said, opening the container and holding up a Chicken Chunx. "And these," he said, grinning, "are the eggs."

Cass burst out laughing. "You're joking!"

"Scout's honor," he said, holding up his fingers in the Boy Scout salute. Cass picked up a piece and bit into it tentatively. "What do you think?" he asked. "Tasty, eh?"

She chewed thoughtfully, swallowed with difficulty, then looked up at him. "Fire the marketing director. You and the other big-shot burger chains should stay in the burger business and get out of the chicken nugget business. None of you has a decent product and you know it."

He shook his head, chuckling. "Cass, you're priceless. We did marketing surveys in ten cities before we introduced Chicken Chunx. Based on those surveys, we think we have a profitable line in Chicken Chunx."

"Maybe surveys don't work." She shrugged. "Or maybe I'm the only person in the country who knows good chicken."

"If you're such an expert on chicken, maybe I should hire you as a consultant."

She arched a brow. "The great Ryan St. James admitting he needs help?" she teased.

"Not on your life. I just think there's no better product in the country."

"You can't really think that, Ryan, not after tasting Uncle Henry's chicken." She picked up a Chicken Chunx. "Maybe we should have a contest," she said thoughtfully. "A taste test or something...."

Ryan chuckled. "You're really a fighter, aren't you, Cass? You'd take on Goliath and plan on winning."

She gave him a knowing look. "You just can't admit it, can you, St. James? You can't admit that it's possible that a two-bit drive-in restaurant can do a better job than the great Burger City chain."

"Cass, if you're planning on getting Chick-O-Rama in the black, I wish you all the luck in the world. As far as I'm concerned, Waterbury is big enough for both of us. My Chicken Chunx won't be hurt by your chicken."

No, Cass thought, but our chicken could be hurt by your burgers.... She turned her head and stared across the street at Chick-O-Rama, sitting there looking like a bedraggled hound. The neon sign was pitiful in the glare of the afternoon sun, the parking lot a mass of cracked tar, choked with weeds and littered with glass. Next to Burger City, it looked pathetic. No wonder so few customers went there any longer. Who would, given a chance to come to a sparkling clean Burger City? No matter how good Uncle Henry's chicken was, if it wasn't presented in an appealing package, it was doomed.

Cass suppressed a sigh. If she let herself think too long, she got discouraged by the prospect of pulling Chick-O-Rama out of the financial doldrums. Hadn't Uncle Henry been threatening to retire one of these days? Maybe she should just give in and let him. She could go back to the supermarket. It might not have been the most glamorous job, but she knew she'd end up a store manager someday....

"Cass," Ryan said. "You still here?"

Startled, she smiled and shook her head. "I'm afraid I was a few miles away, back at the supermarket."

"The supermarket?"

She shredded a napkin, her forehead knotted into worry lines. "Henry's thinking about retiring. I'm not sure I could carry on the business without him."

"What's that got to do with—" Ryan broke off, then nodded knowingly. "Ah. You'd sell out and go back to work as the produce manager, is that it?"

"It's not as bad as it sounds, Ryan. They liked me there. I was the first woman manager of produce. They told me if I ever wanted to come back, I'd be store manager someday."

Ryan watched her, his face troubled. "I can't believe you'd do that, Cass," he said finally. "Just like I can't believe you dropped out of Yale because of a man."

"It wasn't because of a man!" she said hotly. "I'd flunked a course and didn't have enough credits to graduate."

Ryan shook his head. "I'm disappointed in you, Cass Dickens. You're never going to get anywhere if you keep lying to yourself."

"Lying to myself!" Cass's face burned. "Where do you get off talking to me like that? You don't know me enough to put in your two cents' worth of therapy." She was about to get up, but Ryan reached out and took her hand.

"You dropped out of Yale because of what happened with Geoff, and now you're thinking of giving up on Chick-O-Rama because you might not have Uncle Henry there for support. When are you going to realize you can only rely on yourself in this life?"

Cass stared at him, then pulled her hand from his grip. "If I need your advice, St. James, I'll come asking for it. Until I do, keep it to yourself."

He watched her with sad eyes, shaking his head slightly. "You really do remind me of myself," he said, almost as if he were talking to himself. "The same obstinate pride, the same inability to listen to the voice of reason. There's only one difference."

Despite herself, she was interested. "What's that?"

"I never gave up."

She stared at him a minute, taking in the full implication of his words, then catapulted from the booth. But Ryan was right behind her. She walked determinedly through the restaurant, ignoring his presence, her chin up, her heels clicking rapidly on the tile floor. When she pushed open the sparkling glass doors, the humid air hit her with the force of a prizefighter's punch.

"Are you going to talk to me?" Ryan asked from next to her. "Or are you just planning to go away mad?"

"I don't give up!" she said, whirling to face him, eyes blazing, hands clenched into fists.

"No?"

"No!"

He lifted one side of his mouth in amusement. "Then why are you running away right now?"

"I'm not running away!" He just lifted an eyebrow. She looked away, unable to stand what she saw in those taunting blue eyes. "I'm not running away," she said again, her voice quieter this time. She felt tired and she knew she couldn't keep up the act any longer. Ryan was right; she'd been running from lots of things for too long.

Ryan reached out and touched her hair, letting it sift through his fingers. "Don't let anyone or anything stop you from what you want to do, Cass, especially a man, whether the man be your Uncle Henry or me. When you left Yale, you weren't dropping out because you weren't college material, you were letting what happened with a no-account bum get to you. To really prove to him what you were made of, you should have stayed and gotten that degree and then shoved it under his nose, not slunk off as if you were admitting he and his family were right about you." He put a finger under her chin and lifted her face to his.

"And if you really want to make Chick-O-Rama work, then by God, you stay and do it. If Uncle Henry wants to retire, let him, but don't let his wanting to retire be the excuse to stop fighting it out on your own. Don't ever let anyone run your life for you, Cass. Run it yourself, in your own way, and on your own terms."

Cass stared at him, puzzled. Why would Ryan St. James talk to her this way? It didn't make sense—unless he really cared for her. She searched his face, feeling hope rise up inside her. "Why are you telling me this?" she asked. "You're almost encouraging me to stay put and fight Burger City."

He didn't answer right away. He turned and stared across the street at Chick-O-Rama, his face thoughtful. But when he looked back at her, the thoughtfulness was gone, replaced by humor. "If you really want to know, it's because I kinda like the idea of a small chicken restaurant taking on the number-one fast-food chain in the country. I haven't had a challenge in a long time. That little old mess across the street isn't much of a challenge, I'll grant you, but it's better than nothing."

Cass's hopes fell, replaced by slow-burning anger. It was all a silly game with him, an exercise in power. She lifted her chin, green eyes glittering. "Okay," she said coolly. "I'll play your game."

"Oh, no, Cass," he murmured, shaking his head. "It's not a game." He reached out and fingered a strand of her hair. "What we're engaged in is deadly serious."

She frowned. If she didn't know better, she'd almost think he was talking about something else entirely besides business. She shook off his hand and looked away. "Does our new status as business rivals mean we won't be seeing each other on a social basis?"

"Oh, I don't think we have to go *that* far...."

She turned and looked back at him. He was standing with his hands shoved in his pants pockets, his head tilted to the side, grinning at her. She felt her heart turn over. He was so damned attractive. Well, maybe she'd just play a little game of her own.

She widened her eyes. "No?" she asked innocently. "I'm not so sure. Maybe it wouldn't be a good idea to fraternize with the enemy."

"I think we can handle it," he said, putting an arm around her and guiding her toward his car.

Blithely she slipped from under his arm. "I don't know, St. James," she said, putting on a thoughtful frown. "I don't think it's a very good idea."

"You got a better idea?"

She played it for all it was worth. "I think we should stop seeing each other," she said. "After all, you just pumped me up with all that sound business advice. I'd be a fool to let my attraction to you as a man undermine my future, now wouldn't I? I mean, you *did* just tell me in so many words that I shouldn't let a man, *any* man, change the course of my life...."

"But we're not talking about just any man now, are we?"

She faced him with wide, innocent eyes. "Aren't we?"

His grin sent her heart into orbit. He reached out and pulled her into his arms. "No," he murmured, planting a proprietary kiss on her mouth, "we aren't."

She tried to keep the breathlessness out of her voice. "What are we talking about, then?"

His eyes roamed her face, and the look in his eyes took her breath away. Suddenly, his grin was gone and he was completely serious. "We're talking about this particular guy who's crazy about this particular woman," he said, his voice rough with emotion. "We're talking major interest. The guy can't sleep at night unless she's in bed with him, see? The guy's out of control. If she tells him she won't see him again, he won't be responsible for his actions—I mean he might kidnap her or something. Do you see the extent of the problem?"

She tried to speak, but she was filled with incredible yearning. For a moment, she forgot where they were. Every part of her wanted to touch him, with nothing between—no clothes to stand in the way of skin against skin—and she had to shake herself back to reality. "Yeah," she said, her own voice throatier than usual, "I think I see the problem."

"What're we gonna do about it?" he murmured.

She took a shaky breath. She saw nothing but his lips hovering over hers, so near, yet because they were in public, entirely too far. "I think maybe she should go home with him," she whispered, "and see where it all leads...."

She heard his breath escape shakily, then he took her hand. "Yeah," he said, his voice still rough with emotion. "I think that's probably best."

Half an hour later they were in his bed. The ride home had been filled with incredible tension. Luckily, there'd been no police cars out between Waterbury and Woodbury. Now, they lay naked on their sides, facing each other, their bodies not touching. It was sweet torture to lie so close yet not touch.

"Every time I get out of the bed with you," he said, "I swear to myself I'm going to take you out and wine and dine you, but then all I want to do is get back in bed."

She swallowed. "I know." Her voice sounded constricted. Her eyes were large, staring straight into his. "This is all I want, too."

"You think it means we've just got the hots for each other?"

She searched his face. "Do you?"

He shook his head. "No." Slowly, he reached out and traced his finger down her neck, into the hollow of her throat. He placed his open palm on her breast. "No," he said again. "I want to know all about you. Everything. But I want this, too."

She nodded, her eyes closing. She couldn't keep looking at the desire in his face and think straight. She was on fire as it was, her body filled with building tension. She drew in her breath sharply as he began to toy with her nipple.

She drew another deep breath and turned on her back. He came with her, caressing her breasts and parting her pliant legs with his knee. She smiled sensuously as she wrapped her arms around his muscular back. "It was never like this with Geoff," she whispered.

That stopped him. He raised up and stared down into her face. "No?"

She shook her head, her eyes serious. "Something with him was missing. I thought I loved him, but I see now it was just sex. This is..." She broke off, staring up into his dark blue eyes, and realized suddenly what was happening to her.

"This is what?" Ryan coaxed.

She lowered her gaze. She didn't want him to read the answer. "This is better," she said finally.

If he'd expected her to say more, he didn't let on. Yet something about him communicated disappointment. He turned onto his back and stared up at the ceiling. "I was in love once," he said finally. "The only trouble was, I found out she cared more about my money than she did about me."

Cass stared at him. It came as a surprise that any woman would be more interested in Ryan's money than in him. Cass had seen Ryan's money only as a problem, not as a reward. "What happened?"

He rubbed his chest absently, still staring at the ceiling. "Nothing very dramatic. We got engaged and everything seemed fine, but then a lot of little things didn't hit me right. Pretty soon all our conversations seemed to be about what she wanted to buy when we got married. That kinda nagged at me for a while, until one day we had a fight and I was so mad I said some things I shouldn't have."

Cass turned on her side to face him. She wanted to reach out, but was afraid to. Would he understand that it was him she cared for, not his money? "It's ironic, isn't it?" she finally said. "It was money and social position that came between me and Geoff, and almost the same things that parted you and her."

He turned his head and looked at her. "For different reasons, though. You wanted Geoff, not his money. She wanted my money, not me."

"What was the fight about?"

"The fight?"

"The one you had when you realized all she wanted was your money."

Ryan turned his head and looked back at the ceiling. He didn't speak for a long time. "I told her something about myself," he finally said. "I guess she didn't like what she heard. She was one of those women who wanted everything in life to be perfect." He turned his head and looked back at Cass. "Are you like that, Cass Dickens? Do you want everything in life to be perfect, no problems?"

She stared at him, puzzled, not knowing what to say. "I...I don't know what you mean," she said. "But I know there are always going to be problems in life. They're there, almost by definition." She searched his eyes. "What did you tell her, Ryan?"

He just looked at her, as if assessing whether to tell her or not. Finally he shook his head. "Maybe someday I'll tell you. It's not really important. It just seemed to be then."

She wondered if that were true, but knew she couldn't press him. If he wanted to tell her, he would. All she could do was create the atmosphere that would make it easy for him to trust her. She reached out and gently rubbed his arm. "I like you, Ryan," she whispered. "I like you a lot...."

He turned onto his side and pulled her closer. "Yeah?" he asked, smiling. "I kinda like you, too."

She smiled back, for the first time letting her true feelings surface. Who was she trying to kid? She was in love with the man! She wouldn't tell him yet, though. It was too soon, and she still didn't know exactly how he felt about her. If he didn't feel the same, she'd be glad she hadn't made a fool of herself when he walked out of her life.

Twelve

The following week, Cass and Uncle Henry closed Chick-O-Rama for remodeling. They took out a half-page ad in the Waterbury paper, announcing the date of the grand re-opening. There would be a new look, but the same tried and time-tested chicken. And Cass had decided they'd keep the name Chick-O-Rama. Somehow, it fit the place, and Uncle Henry was ecstatic.

Cass was knee-deep in blueprints and sawdust when Ryan found her at Chick-O-Rama that Friday. Wearing a hard hat and dust-covered jeans and shirt, she was directing the demolition of the interior walls.

Uncle Henry grinned at Ryan. "This is supposed to be Cass's vacation; will you get her *out* of here, please?"

Cass whirled around, green eyes flashing, then she spied Ryan. "Oh." She whipped off her hard hat and smoothed back her sweaty hair. Her heart began to beat in pleasurable double time, as it always did when she saw him. "Hi. I didn't hear you come in."

"I guess you wouldn't," Ryan said, grinning. "You were too busy yelling at that poor carpenter."

"Ryan!" she cried, laughing, "are you going to take Uncle Henry's side?"

"Sure am," he said amiably, putting an arm around her. "We're in cahoots. I'm on vacation and your restaurant is closed and Henry claims he doesn't need you here." He lowered his voice, whispering into her ear so only she could hear. "That sounds good to me, because I'm up for a trip to Maine and I was kinda hoping you'd go along."

"To Maine?"

He nodded. "How about it? Think your uncle would mind?"

She looked at Uncle Henry. "Um, Uncle Henry, Ryan invited me to...um...go away for a while. I'd hate to leave you here alone—"

"Go!" her uncle said. "Don't even think twice."

"You wouldn't mind, Uncle Henry?"

"Mind?" He looked at her as if she were crazy. "Mind a chance to rebuild this place the way the architect planned it, without you sticking your two cents in every five minutes? It'd be a pleasure."

Ryan's eyes gleamed at her. "Then I guess it's settled. It'll take about seven hours to get there. I've got a room reserved at an inn for the next week. I'll pick you up in a couple hours. Think you can be ready?"

She couldn't contain her happiness. An entire week in Maine, alone with Ryan in a romantic country inn. What could be more perfect? "I'll be ready," she said, her eyes shining.

"I can't wait," he murmured under his breath.

"Me either," she whispered back.

Uncle Henry rolled his eyes at them. "Will you two love-birds just get outta here, please?"

Laughing, Cass threw her arms around Henry and hugged him hard. Today, she was in love with the world. Nothing could go wrong. As long as she was with Ryan, everything was perfect.

On Saturday night, a week after they'd arrived in Maine, they sat on the inn's veranda, holding hands as they looked out at the whitecapped ocean that crashed against the rocky coast. The sun stained the sky in the west, casting brilliantly colored streamers over the water.

"I don't want to leave, Cass," Ryan said. "I haven't relaxed like this since I was a kid. It's been the best vacation I've ever had."

"Me too," she said, smiling dreamily. Her long hair fluttered gently in the breeze. Her skin had bronzed in the past week and she was entirely at ease, abloom with the love she felt for Ryan. "I can't remember when I've been so happy, Ryan."

He pressed her hand. "I'm going to make sure I keep on making you happy, Cass," he said. "I only wish I didn't have to go back to work so soon."

"Will you move back to your apartment in New York?"

For the first time in a week, he frowned. "I'll have to. There are bound to be problems at work when I get back—there always are. But I'll come back to Woodbury every weekend."

"You better," she warned, grinning at him as she teased, "or I'll come and get you."

"Now why is that exactly the kind of threat I like?" he asked, grinning.

She felt her lips tremble with another smile, felt everything inside her rise up in contentment and joy. After just a week in Ryan's presence, she felt as if she were almost standing on firm ground. Their relationship had progressed to the point that she felt more secure than she ever had before. Ryan was everything she'd ever wanted in a man—sensitive, humorous, strong, loving. Sitting here on the porch, Cass felt she had everything she'd ever wanted.

Except one thing. Ryan had shown her in a million ways that he cared for her, but as unreasonable as it seemed, she wanted him to say the words.

That night, they left the restaurant where they'd shared a formal, candlelit dinner and drove back to the inn and went quickly to their room. When they closed the door, they were in each other's arms. No words were spoken—none were needed. Everything was said with lips and tongues and hands. They undressed hurriedly, fingers shaking, and fell onto the bed. In their haste and their desire for each other, Ryan forgot to use protection.

Somehow, that made their lovemaking even more wonderful for Cass. Finally, he'd wanted her so much that even the specter of getting her pregnant hadn't worried him. Not that she would—it was a safe time for her. She knew it was irrational, but, somehow, this made her feel that Ryan really cared for her.

She turned into his arms and nuzzled her lips against his chest. "I like making love this way with you," she whispered. "I know it sounds silly, but it's even more intimate somehow."

Ryan looked puzzled for a minute. "What are you talking about?" he asked, chuckling lazily as he rubbed his hand up and down her silken back.

She laughed shortly. "How quickly they forget!" she teased. "This is the first time we haven't used protection, Ryan."

He propped himself up on his elbow and looked down at her, his eyes shadowed. "Is this a bad time for you? I mean, there isn't a chance you could get pregnant, is there?"

"There shouldn't be any problems," she said slowly. She knew she should appreciate his sense of responsibility and concern, but all that she could see was his fear of being "trapped," all that she could feel was a sense of distance and rejection. But she forced herself to reassure him that it was a safe time. She knew she wasn't being fair, but she was unable to stop herself from feeling the way she did. "If we were going to slip up, this was the safest time."

Ryan lay back down, still looking worried. "Are you absolutely positive, Cass?"

She lay looking at him, her eyes mirroring her pain. Her first impulse was to get up and walk away, to put as much physical distance between herself and Ryan as she could, but that was foolish. Ryan had shown her that she always ran away from problems, and she wasn't going to now. Somehow she had to overcome the impulse to jump to conclusions and she had to talk about this. But maybe Ryan was more like Geoff than she'd thought.

Reaching out, she gently touched his arm. "Sharing this last week has made me feel so close to you, Ryan. Somehow, it hurts when you react this way."

Ryan lay staring at the ceiling, a muscle working in his jaw. "You don't understand, Cass."

"That's right," she said, her grip on her anger beginning to falter. "I don't. Maybe you could tell me what's going on, Ryan, instead of shutting me out."

Ryan closed his eyes and ran a tired hand over his face. "It's just that I don't want anything to ruin what we have, Cass."

She stared at him, tormented. "What *do* we have, Ryan? A pleasant week-in-the-sun relationship that will end when you go back to work?"

He opened his eyes and looked at her, that muscle still working his cheek. "No. What we have is special. You know that and so do I, but if you got pregnant right now, it could ruin everything."

"That's right," she said, getting up hurriedly and searching for her clothing. "You'd suddenly be stuck with a woman who wanted to marry you, and marriage is the farthest thing from your mind, isn't it?"

"Cass." He stood and put his hands on her upper arms. "Stop it. You know that's not how I feel."

"No, Ryan, I don't know that," she said quietly. "I don't know how you feel at all because you won't tell me. For a while I thought I knew what you felt from the way things were between us—but now I don't have a clue what's going on inside you."

They stood staring at each other, then Ryan released her and ran his hand back through his hair distractedly. "I just want to give us the chance we deserve, Cass."

"How can we have a chance when you won't *talk* to me, Ryan?" she asked softly.

He searched her eyes, and seemed to debate with himself. Finally, he heaved a tired sigh. "I've seen too many people trapped into marrying—good people who thought they loved each other, who couldn't handle the pressures of marriage and parenthood at the same time." He looked away, his eyes haunted. "And the kids produced, what about them?" He shook his head. "I don't want to bring any children into the world who aren't the product of a strong, secure marriage, Cass."

Watching him, she felt a deep spasm of alarm. His face was implacable. She suddenly saw why he was so successful—determination glittered in his eyes, was stamped in the thin, taut line of his mouth. If the gods tried to rule this man, he'd shake his fist at them and refuse their injunctions. He made his own destiny and nothing would stand in the way of what he wanted.

She looked away, troubled by her insight into Ryan's character. There was still so much she didn't know about him, and there was still a wall between them. What had happened to him to make him feel this way? Somehow, she couldn't ask. If he didn't want to tell her, she couldn't pry. There was a time for questions, and there was a time for silence. "I'm going to take a shower," she said quietly.

In the bathroom, she stood absently under the steady stream, unaware of the drumming pressure of the water. Would she ever know Ryan St. James? Would she ever trust her instincts enough to be able to tell if he truly cared about her? This past week had seemed so wonderful, yet tonight everything had come apart.

She stepped from the shower and looked at herself in the mirror. Why was he so frightened of getting her pregnant? Was it because, like Geoff, he didn't want to get involved, or could there be another explanation? She frowned thoughtfully and began to dry herself off. Tomorrow, she'd broach the subject again. Somehow, she'd have to get him to open up and talk to her. Only then would she be able to fully trust Ryan.

But their fight cast a pall over their last day together. Or perhaps it was just the knowledge that their time together was ending. As they drove home toward Connecticut, Ryan brought up the subject of her going back to school.

"Why are you so interested in my education?" she asked irritably. She didn't give a hoot about her lack of a college degree. Right now, she and Ryan had more important things to discuss. She tapped her fingers on the Sunday *New York Times* in her lap, then held up the front section, a clear message to Ryan that she didn't want to discuss her incomplete degree.

"Will you put that paper down?" he asked, reaching out to take it from her and thrusting it behind them. "I'm interested because I care about you," he said, sounding as if he didn't care about her at all. Frankly, he merely sounded angry. "I hate to see you throw away your future by refusing to get a degree. Women find it hard enough in the working world today without sentencing themselves to working in low-paying jobs. And that's exactly what you're doing, Cass."

She stared at him, her temper simmering. Here he was talking about her future in the work force when she wanted to talk about something a lot more serious—their future together as a couple. What right did he have to grab the paper from her hands? If she wanted to read the paper, she'd read it! She turned around and picked it up. "My going back to school would make it simple for you, wouldn't it, Ryan?" she shot back, saying the first thing that came into her head. "I'd be out of the picture and you'd get to buy Chick-O-Rama from Henry, and that eyesore, as you call it, would be gone."

"For crying out loud, Cass," he said. "What in heaven's name would I want with Chick-O-Rama? You're not even thinking straight." He glared at her and snatched the paper from her hands again. "Dammit, Cass, the least you can do when we're fighting is pay attention to me!"

She snatched the paper back. "Maybe I don't want to fight," she said. "Maybe I'd rather see what's on TV tonight." Actually, she couldn't care less about the television schedule, but she burrowed through the mammoth *Times*, determined to have her own way.

"Cass." Something about his voice was different. He didn't sound angry anymore, he sounded almost loving. She looked up and saw that he was watching her with apologetic eyes. "I don't want to fight either, honey," he said, reaching out and squeezing her hand.

Suddenly, reading the paper didn't seem very important anymore and she let it slide to the floor. "I guess I don't really want to read the paper very much," she murmured, smiling.

"Good," he said, taking his eyes off the road long enough to lean over and kiss her. "I'm selfish when it comes to you, Cass. I want all your attention for myself."

"Oh, Ryan," she said, "I'm sorry. I was being childish."

"No more than me," he said. "I'm sorry, too." He sighed as he looked at the cars that whizzed by them on I-95. "This past week has been wonderful, Cass. I wish it didn't have to end. I'll be going back to work tomorrow and I don't want to face it. Al Fletcher, my marketing director, will have a report for me and if the rumblings are true, there'll be a flood of problems to solve." He sighed and squeezed her hand again. "Sometimes I think I'd like to get out of the burger business and just take you away to a South Sea island somewhere and live on love."

Love. It was the first time he'd used the word, and while he hadn't exactly used it to tell her he loved her, the signs were promising. She inched down in the plush leather seat and smiled at him. "What would you do if I called your bluff, big guy?" she teased. "What if I told you that's exactly what I'd like to do—go to a remote island and live on love?"

He looked at her, his blue eyes surprisingly serious. "I have a feeling we'd do pretty well together on an island somewhere, Cass. This past week in Maine proved that. No, the real test will be if we can get along in the real world, with the pressures of our businesses and personal lives to contend with."

He was right, she thought, but she wasn't worried about fitting him in. She was much more concerned about his ability to find time for her once he returned to his demanding job and the pressure of heading a large corporation like Burger City. "I think I'll always be able to find time for you, Ryan," she said quietly. "I just hope you'll be able to find time for me."

"Always, Cass," he said, squeezing her hand again. "I'll always find time for you."

Reassured, she touched his arm. "I'm sorry for fighting with you earlier," she said softly. "I guess I'm just defensive about dropping out of school. You and Henry keep barking at me to go back and I know I should, but I just keep putting it off."

He smiled at her, covering her hand with his. "One of these days, you will, Cass."

"Yes," she said slowly, "I might get my degree someday, but that doesn't mean I'll desert Chick-O-Rama. I'll make that place work if it's the last thing I do."

"Those sound like fighting words, Cass," he said, chuckling. "If there's one thing I like better than a good fight, it's a good fighter."

She arched a wry brow. "Even if the fighter is fighting you?"

"Especially then," he said. "There's nothing like a little spice in a relationship."

Cass frowned thoughtfully at the greenery that whizzed by. If she hadn't vowed to fight for Chick-O-Rama on the first day she met Ryan, would he have even been attracted to her? Was it the idea of fighting off business competition that appealed to him, or was he truly interested in her as a woman?

She tried to shake off her questions. Hadn't this last week with him proved where his interest lay? She rested her head against the back of the seat. He hadn't even wanted to turn on a television or read a newspaper; he'd said he didn't want to be distracted by business. He'd only wanted to be with her.

Feeling better, she turned her head and looked at Ryan, who turned at that moment and smiled at her. Sudden happiness flowered inside her. She was foolish to continue doubting Ryan's interest in her.

She asked him to come in when he brought her home, but he shook his head. "I'm afraid I can't, Cass. I've got to spend some time preparing for work. There's a meeting tomorrow with the Marketing Department, and I need to go over the report Al sent me last week."

He carried her bag in, then she walked back to the car with him and put her arms around him. "You're sure you can't come in?"

He kissed her lingeringly. "No," he said, sounding a little hoarse when the kiss ended. "I'm not sure. And if you kiss me like that again, I'll be in trouble. I'll want to stay with you all night. Unfortunately, I've got to leave."

That was all she needed—affirmation that he wanted to be with her, even though duty called. She stepped back. "Then get going, Ryan. Far be it from me to come between a man and his work."

"You do, though, Cass Dickens," he said with a grin. "When I was at work all week after I first met you, I couldn't even think straight. I couldn't concentrate on anything. That's when I knew I had to take some time off to be with you."

"Do you think you got me out of your system?" she teased.

He didn't grin back at her. Instead, entirely serious, he pulled her into his arms. "No," he said huskily, "I didn't get you out of my system at all. If anything, I got you more deeply embedded in my life." He kissed her hungrily, then rested his forehead against hers. "I'll call you tomorrow night from New York."

She nodded, her heart beating rapidly, her breathing constricted. "Okay. I'll be thinking about you."

"Mm," he murmured, kissing her. "And me about you."

"Good night, Ryan," she whispered.

He kissed her again, running his hands up and down her back. "Good night, honey." He took a deep breath, and seemed about to release her, but instead he tightened his arms around her. "Cass, I don't want to let you go."

"I know," she whispered. "I want you to stay, too."

He kissed her again, then said, "There's so much I want to tell you, Cass. So much I haven't shared with you. But I will, honey, as soon as I get the mess at the office straightened out. I've purposely been blocking work out, but now I have to deal with it. As soon as I do, I'll be back. We'll talk then, and get some things settled between us." He kissed her again. "Lord," he said when the kiss ended. "I wish I could stay with you tonight."

Taking a deep breath, she pushed out of his arms. "Go," she commanded. "You've got work to do." She turned and scooped up the paper from the car seat, then slammed the door shut. "And I'll read the paper. Otherwise, I wouldn't be able to get to sleep from missing you so much."

Ryan kissed her softly. "I'll call," he murmured.

They paused, looking into each other's eyes, then she bolted from the driveway and raced into the house, not stopping to look back. She waited until she heard his car engine, then turned and pressed her nose to the glass and watched him drive away, her heart full. She loved him so much.

Thirteen

———

Half an hour later, Cass stared at the headline in the paper: BURGER KINGDOM CROWS OVER VICTORY—CHICKEN NIBBLES TRIUMPH IN NATIONWIDE SURVEY. She rattled the pages, folded the paper back, and began to read:

A nationwide survey shows that consumers prefer Burger Kingdom's Chicken Nibbles two to one over all other chicken products sold by burger chains. Hugo Lattimore, President of the nationwide Burger Kingdom chain, is claiming victory in the chicken wars. "The other chains will be faced with a major decision after they see the results of this survey," Lattimore said in an interview in his Chicago headquarters. "I wouldn't be surprised if some of them drop their chicken products. One thing's for sure—they'll at least try to improve them to meet the challenge of our superior Chicken Nibbles.''

Pressed for clarification, Lattimore stated Burger Kingdom had bought the secret recipe for their Chicken Nibbles from a small chicken restaurant chain in the Midwest. ''After all,'' Lattimore said, ''I'm a burger man. What do I know about chicken? When I stumbled on a good product in Nebraska, I bought the chain and got the recipe. If it worked for me, it could work for others.'' He cited Heublein Corporation's acquisition of Colonel Sanders' chicken chain some years back as the example that caused him to decide to add chicken to the menu of his thriving Burger Kingdom chain.

There had been speculation that Burger City would refuse to join the chicken wars, but three months ago that speculation was put to rest when they introduced their Chicken Chunx with a multimillion dollar advertising campaign. At the opening of his thousandth restaurant in Waterbury, CT, last month, Burger City founder Ryan St. James was quoted as saying, ''Our new Chicken Chunx are superior to any other chicken product on the market.'' St. James was unavailable for comment late last week. Burger City marketing director Allen Fletcher would only say St. James had been apprised of the consumer survey weeks ago, and would be issuing a statement within the week.

Cass stared at the article, then lifted puzzled eyes. ''Weeks ago?'' she said out loud. ''He knew *weeks* ago?'' She threw the paper aside and sat back, trying to make sense of the article and what it meant. Her green eyes clouded. Was it possible after all that Ryan really *did* want to buy them out? She groaned. Had Ryan found out that Henry Dickens had a good product but was in financial trouble? Was that why he'd come to the opening of the Waterbury Burger City?

He'd never gone to a grand opening before. Why had he chosen Waterbury? Ostensibly, he'd come because it was the thousandth restaurant in his chain. Why hadn't he done that for the opening of his one hundredth restaurant, his five hundredth, his seven-hundred-fiftieth?

Overwhelmed by doubt, she picked up the article and read Lattimore's words again: "When I stumbled on a good product in Nebraska, I bought the chain and got the recipe. If it worked for me, it could work for others." Cass felt herself begin to tremble. She pressed the article to her bosom and told herself she was making mountains out of those damned little molehills.

But there were more questions. The more she thought about it the more evidence against Ryan seemed to accumulate. Why had Ryan been so adamant about not reading newspapers or watching television when they were in Maine? He'd said he didn't want to be distracted by business, but could it have been that he didn't want *her* to read the papers and find out about the survey?

She gnawed on her thumbnail the same way her doubts attacked her feelings for Ryan. He hadn't wanted her to read the paper today on the way home, either. Was that because he wanted to close a deal with Henry before she had a chance to find out what was going on? And then there was Saturday night, and Ryan's fear of her getting pregnant....

Cass lay back on the couch, feeling sick. As much as she wanted to believe Ryan, the seeds of doubt had been planted in her years before, after her experience with Geoffrey Sutton. Now they seemed to have grown to fruition—she couldn't trust any man, she couldn't even trust her own instincts. She pressed her knuckles to her eyes and tried to remember what Ryan had said a week or so ago, about how she always ran away. Was jumping to conclusions about Ryan just another form of running away? If she didn't give him the benefit of the doubt, if she didn't at least talk to him, wouldn't she be guilty of running away from problems?

She opened her eyes and stared at the phone. She'd call him. Before even another minute went by, she'd talk to him and clear all this up. It was probably all in her imagination anyway. She chuckled sardonically to herself. She had a habit of building things up until they took on proportions that didn't have anything to do with reality. With trembling fingers, she dialed Ryan's number.

The phone rang ten times before she hung up. Frowning, she glanced at the clock. It was just after five p.m. He'd dropped her off almost an hour ago. That was plenty of time to get home. She took a shaky breath and told herself he was in the shower. Yes, that was it. She'd call again in a few minutes, and talk with him then.

Ryan ran his finger down the names in the phone book—DiCioccio, Dick, Dicken, Dickens. C. Dickens. He smiled at Cass's number and looked at the name beneath it—Henry Dickens. Putting a dime in the slot, he dialed the number. It was hot in the stifling little booth, so he kept the door open, his eyes on the new exterior of Chick-O-Rama. He'd driven by, hoping to find Henry, but the place was closed up tight. He should have known. It was Sunday afternoon, and the restaurant wasn't scheduled to open for another week.

Suddenly Henry answered, sounding sleepy, as if he'd been awakened from a nap. "H'lo?"

"Henry, this is Ryan St. James. Did I wake you?"

"Ryan!" Henry said, sounding pleased. "Yeah, I fell asleep watching the Mets game." He chuckled, then seemed to come fully awake. "Hey! Nothing's wrong, is it? I mean, is Cass okay?"

"Cass is fine," Ryan said, smiling. "In fact, she's better than fine—she's wonderful. That's why I called, Henry. I wanted to tell you everything went well. I think Cass finally believes that I'm not interested in buying you out, but I'd appreciate it if you'd continue to keep quiet about that loan I gave you. If she found out, she might just leap to the wrong conclusion again. I'd rather she continues to think it was from the bank."

Henry chuckled. "No problem, Ryan. I'm glad it went well this week, son. Cass is a fine woman, but she needs to learn a few things about life. I guess I kinda hope she'll learn 'em from you."

Ryan shook his head, his eyes suddenly shadowed. "She won't learn from *me*, Henry. I'm the last one to try to give lessons about life."

Henry chuckled again. "Maybe you two can learn together, then. Glad everything went well. The renovations are coming along just fine. I never did properly thank you for that loan." His voice grew gruff, as if thank-you's came hard to Henry Dickens. "It meant a lot, Ryan."

"Thanks, Henry." He smiled, warmed by the older man's gratitude. "I have some business waiting for me in New York, so I have to go. I'm on my way there now, but I'll be seeing you soon." He hung up, then considered the phone thoughtfully.

There was so much he hadn't told Cass. What would she do if she found out the truth about him? All his life, people had rejected him because of what he was. Now he realized he hadn't played fair and square. She'd told him about Geoff, yet he'd withheld practically everything about himself from her.

He shook his head at himself. A while back, he'd accused Cass of running away from problems. Now he wondered if that wasn't exactly what he'd been doing all his life. There was only one difference between him and Cass—he'd chosen to run away by being successful; Cass ran away by making sure she never would be.

* * *

Cass stared at her demolished thumbnail. She looked back at the clock. Five-thirty and Ryan still wasn't home. He'd probably stopped to get a bite to eat. Somehow she'd overcome her initial fears and talked herself into believing in Ryan, yet nervous flutters remained in her stomach. She told herself that was normal—she was new to love, and hadn't gotten the hang of it yet.

On impulse, she decided to call Uncle Henry. She'd been so wrapped up in Ryan all week in Maine, she hadn't even thought to call Henry and ask how the work on Chick-O-Rama was going. She smiled as she dialed. He was probably just as glad she hadn't called. When he answered, he sounded happy.

"Henry?" she said, smiling. "It's me. I'm back."

"Yeah, I know," he said.

She frowned. "You do?"

There was an uneasy silence, then he stumbled over his words. "Well, um..." Suddenly he brightened, sounding just like a schoolboy who'd found an excuse for a lie. "Hey, you're callin' me, aren't you? Course I know you're back!"

Her frown deepened as she tried to figure out why Henry sounded so guilty. "Yes," she muttered doubtfully, then shrugged. "Henry, I had a wonderful time in Maine."

"Oh? Did you guys do anything special?"

"No," she said, "we just hung around and ate lobster a lot." She glanced at the clock. "I thought I'd call you. Ryan dropped me off about an hour and a half ago, but he's not home yet." She frowned. "I'm getting worried, Henry."

"Oh, you don't have to worry, Cassie," Henry said. "He's on his way to New York."

She stared at the phone. "He is."

"Uh... well... I mean he *probably* is."

"But you sounded as if you knew," she persisted. Something wasn't right. She knew Henry like a beloved book. When he stammered like that, he was hiding something.

"How would *I* know?" Henry asked.

She could almost see those shaggy eyebrows of his, rising over widened eyes that could never fool her. She tapped a perturbed finger on the phone. "*That's* what I want to know," she said, sounding stern. If she put enough iron in her voice, she could always bluff him into telling her what was going on.

"Oh, Cassie," Henry said. "I know because he called me, for cryin' out loud."

"He called you?" She sat up. Why would Ryan call Henry? In the next moment, her heart seemed to stop and her mouth went dry. "He *called* you?"

Henry groaned. "Come on, Cass, there isn't any law against a man callin' me, is there?"

"Why'd he call, Uncle Henry?" she demanded sternly.

There was silence a moment, then he said, "He called to talk business."

"Business! He called to talk *business* with you?" Her worst fears were coming true. It was like a nightmare. She'd gnawed a damned thumbnail off trying to give Ryan the benefit of the doubt, and look where she was now. "We're not selling, Henry," she said, her voice trembling. "Do you hear me? We're not selling."

"Who said anything about selling?" Henry said, sounding peeved. Was he peeved at her or himself? That was the question.

"Isn't that why Ryan called you?"

"No!"

"Well, you said he called to talk about business."

"You'd worm an apple out of Eve's hand, Cass."

Cass closed her eyes. "Why'd he call you, Henry?"

"He called to tell me he had a good time with you this week!" Henry snapped.

"Oh, sure," Cass said sarcastically, "and I'll bet he calls to give you the stock quotations every day, too."

She heard a minor explosion from the other end of the phone. "You just won't believe in him, will you, Cassie?"

"Well, have you read the papers lately?" she asked hotly. "Henry, I *want* to believe in him, but the evidence against him just keeps piling up. I just finished reading an article in the *New York Times* that says Chicken Chunx are in trouble, and I call you to talk and I find out none other than Ryan St. James himself, founder of the chain that sells Chicken Chunx, has called you. He's met you *twice*, Henry! That's hardly grounds to become bosom buddies! And when I ask you why he called, you finally admit he called to talk business! What would *you* think, Henry?" She broke off, so upset she couldn't think straight.

There was another uneasy silence on the other end of the phone. "Never mind," Henry said, sounding miserable. "Just never mind. I said the wrong thing, that's all."

"Oh, Henry," she said softly, feeling sicker by the minute. "You never could lie. You're trying to keep something from me, I know you are. Please tell me what it's all about."

"Cassie," Henry said, sounding even more upset. "I can't. I just can't, honey."

Cass put a trembling hand to her mouth. "Henry," she whispered, trying to hold back tears. "Please don't sell."

Henry groaned. "Oh, Cassie, this doesn't have anything to do with selling the business. Believe me."

"How can I believe you if you won't tell me what it *is* about?"

Henry sighed mightily. There was a long silence, in which he must have been pondering what to tell her. Finally, he said, "Cassie, I didn't want to tell you this..."

Her heart constricted painfully. She squeezed her eyes shut. "Tell me what?" she asked in a small voice.

"Cassie, Ryan gave me that loan."

Slowly, her eyes opened and she stared sightlessly at the wall. "He what?" This was a true curveball, coming from out of nowhere when she least expected it.

"Now, Cass, it's not like it sounds. That day Ryan came in to see you at the restaurant, when we got to talkin', he told me we needed an infusion of capital or something like that. I didn't tell you this, honey, but I'd already gone to the bank and they'd turned down our loan request. They said we weren't a good financial risk." Henry harrumphed. "So I told Ryan that and he offered to talk to his lawyers and . . ." Henry stopped. "You still there, Cass?"

"I'm here, Henry," she said. She felt old and tired and completely betrayed. It was worse than she'd expected. Her world was crumbling and the two men she loved most on earth were conspiring against her. "Henry, did Ryan ask you not to tell me all this?"

Another uneasy silence, followed by a tired sigh. "Yes."

"Henry," Cass said softly, her heart breaking. "Don't you see why? Henry, he's setting us up. If our business fails, he'll be able to take it over."

"No!" Henry protested vehemently. "It's not like that at all, Cassie."

"All right," she said, sighing, "maybe it isn't. Maybe you're right and Ryan gave you the loan with no strings attached." She broke off, trying to articulate why she felt so betrayed. "But Henry, I deserved to be *told*. Granted, I'm not a full partner, but I *do* own a part of that business, Henry. But you and Ryan—you treated me as if I'm just some feather-headed nincompoop, as if my thoughts and opinions aren't even worth considering."

Henry was silent a moment. "I'm sorry, Cassie. I never thought of it that way, and I don't think Ryan did either. He just knew you didn't trust him. I think maybe he thought this way he'd be showing you he wanted the business to succeed."

Cass rubbed her eyes tiredly. "Either way, Uncle Henry, all it says is that neither of you took me seriously." She sat up, her expression set. "Well, one thing's for certain, no matter what Ryan's motives are, we can't let Chick-O-Rama fail."

"That's right, Cassie," Henry said softly. "We won't let it."

Why did Henry sound so sad? Cass fought back the tears that threatened to erupt. "I'll see you tomorrow Uncle Henry," she said tiredly. She hung up, then sat quietly.

Until this moment, she'd thought she would be taken seriously if she showed how serious she was about keeping Chick-O-Rama solvent. Now she saw that she needed the skills necessary to manage a business. Ryan had been right—when she'd dropped out of Yale, she'd cut off her nose to spite her face. For the first time, she realized that she'd have to get serious herself if she expected anyone else to take her seriously.

She took a deep breath. She was going out for a nice brisk walk. She needed to get out in the fresh air and clear her head so she could think things over. She fed Puss, then set out. Compared to Maine, Connecticut was stifling. For a moment, she felt a pang as she remembered the past week, then she pushed the thought from her mind. She would find out from Ryan what all this was about, but until she did, she wasn't going to let a man ruin her life the way Geoff Sutton almost had. No matter what else he'd done, Ryan had given her good advice. She would find out about going back to school tomorrow. Perhaps she could go to the University of Bridgeport, or Fairfield University. She only needed a few credits to get her degree. Somehow she'd work it out.

And, she'd work it out without abandoning Chick-O-Rama either. The restaurant might have been her uncle's baby once, but it was now hers. If it was the last thing she ever did, she'd make a success of it....

The phone was ringing when Cass returned from her walk. When she answered, Ryan said, "You've been out. I've been calling for over an hour."

She sat down abruptly. Faced with talking to him, she didn't know what to say. "I went for a walk."

"I was worried about you."

She felt herself grow cold with anger. "Were you? What worried you most, Ryan? Not having someone to sleep with tonight, or wondering when our business will fail so you can take over Uncle Henry's recipe?" She knew she was starting the conversation off badly, but she just couldn't help herself.

For a moment, there was complete silence, then he said, "How did you find out?"

"Uncle Henry told me."

"When?"

"A little while ago."

"It's not what you think, Cass."

"Isn't it?" She felt her throat close up. What fabulous story would he concoct to placate her? For a minute, she wanted to hang up, then she remembered that Ryan had told her she always ran away. She took a deep breath. "What is it, then, Ryan? A friendly little loan out of the goodness of your heart?"

"Cass," he said, sounding sad and angry at the same time. "Honey, I know it looks bad, but you've got to believe me."

"How can I?" she cried, tears glittering in her eyes. Suddenly the words were tumbling out. "Ryan, I read an article in the paper a little while ago that said Chicken Chunx are in trouble. They interviewed the head of Burger Kingdom and he said he'd bought a little chicken restaurant in Nebraska and used their recipe and—"

"Cass," Ryan interrupted. "I'm not trying to take over Chick-O-Rama. You've got to believe that."

She tried to keep from trembling. "That's just it, Ryan," she said. "I'm not very good at believing in rich men."

"I know you're not," he said, sounding angry. "I wish I could come over there now and straighten out this mess, but I'm in New York already. I have to straighten one out here first. I just read the report that Al sent me last week and I—"

"You just read it?"

"Yes, that's why I called. I'll call you tomorrow night, the minute I get in from work."

"Don't bother," she snapped. "In the paper, Allen Fletcher said you've known about the report for weeks. Don't lie to me, Ryan. I don't want to hear it."

"He *what*?"

"It's right here in the *Times*," she said, and began reading out loud.

When she finished, Ryan said, "Cass, he did send me a report a couple weeks ago, but I didn't read it. I imagine he thought I did, because I always read reports the minute I get them."

"And this time you didn't," Cass said sarcastically.

"Exactly," he said. "I was too busy thinking about you to pay attention to some damned report."

"And I suppose you expect me to believe that?"

"Cass," he said. "If you don't, there's no hope for us."

Cass played with the telephone cord. Something about his voice told her he wasn't lying. "All right," she said slowly, "maybe you didn't read the report, but you *did* loan Uncle Henry the money. You can't deny that."

"No, and I wouldn't try. But loaning him money doesn't mean I want to buy him out. If anything, it means I hope it succeeds."

"But don't you *see*?" she cried. "You went behind my back, Ryan! How do you think that looks? Don't you think I have reason to doubt you?"

"Yes," he said, sounding tired. "You do. I made a lot of mistakes, Cass, and as soon as I can get back from New York, I'll talk with you, I promise."

"You'll have to talk fast," she said, "because I'm not in the mood to listen very long."

Ryan's chuckle came across the phone lines, surprising her. "Okay, Cass, I'll talk so fast your ears will spin. Then maybe we can get on with our future."

Future? Cass told herself not to even hope. How could she and Ryan have a future, when the present was such a mess?

Fourteen

Red, white, and blue paper bunting hung from the new exterior of Chick-O-Rama, a Sousa march played on the loudspeaker, and Uncle Henry and two newly hired assistants were bustling about the sparkling kitchen as Cass hoisted her sign and waved to a passing motorist. She was dressed in the dreaded chicken outfit again, and either it or the full-page ad in this morning's paper were working. The restaurant had been open only a few hours and business was booming. Cass remembered the ad she'd placed in that morning's paper: "COME ON OVER TO CHICK-O-RAMA," the ad read, "HOME OF THE BEST FRIED CHICKEN IN TOWN." In smaller letters, the ad said "Meet Charlie the Cheerful Chicken!" and then went on to proclaim a "Chicken Challenge: We're having a taste test. Compare Uncle Henry's chicken to all other chicken products from any famous burger joint. If you don't like ours better, we'll refund your money."

It was a daring gimmick, but so far it had paid off. Cass tugged at the bottom of her bulbous chicken outfit, remembering the last time she'd rented this outlandish costume and worn it. How ironic life was. She should have been whooping it up for joy at the success of the grand reopening of Chick-O-Rama, but instead all she could think of was the day she'd first met Ryan.

She glanced back at the newly paved parking lot, packed with cars. Ryan hadn't called her since that Sunday a week ago. She supposed that proved he hadn't been interested in a serious relationship, yet something in her remained doggedly hopeful, despite her resolve not to hope.

But it wouldn't do any good to stand around and feel sorry for herself—she had a job to do. She raised the placard and waved cheerfully to another passing car. Under her mask, she grimaced. The last time she'd worn this ridiculous getup, she'd fainted from the heat. Now, the dog days of summer were over. Fall would be here soon, turning the leaves into a gaudy spectacle and sharpening the air with the scent of cider and apples.

She'd also be going back to school. She'd arranged with Uncle Henry to cut down her hours, so she could attend part-time classes at the University of Bridgeport, majoring in business. She'd have to go a couple more semesters now to get her degree, but it would be worth it. When she was finished, she'd have a degree in Business Administration, and the skills to keep Chick-O-Rama financially solvent, and permanently out of Ryan St. James's hands.

She hoisted her sign high above her head and strode briskly down the street, waving at the kids who cheered and yelled at her. She groaned under her mask at the teenagers whose wolf whistles greeted her appearance. Cars honked and families laughed as she stood on the side of the road, gesturing at the cars that pulled into Burger City's lot across the street, inviting them to come on over to Chick-O-Rama.

Then she spied a motorcycle approaching and felt her heart lurch expectantly. She knew immediately it was Ryan. She watched as he swung the cycle in a wide arc and roared up beside her, gunning his engine. He came to a stop and steadied himself with his feet, then took off his helmet. Her heart softened when she saw how tired he looked.

"I'd know those legs anywhere," he said. "When do you get off?"

"I'm almost done," she said, her voice muffled through her mask. "But that doesn't mean I'm going anywhere with you." She turned on her heel, but he cut the engine on his cycle and got off and followed her.

"You're not?"

"No, I'm not. Henry might need me."

"What if I need you more?"

His quiet question startled her. She turned and stared at him. Fear and hope warred within her. "You mean you need my business, don't you, Mr. St. James?"

He shook his head. "I mean I need *you*. I've been miserable this past week without you."

"There are phones in New York," she said coolly. "You could have called."

"I did," he said. "You were never home when I tried to reach you."

She hesitated. She *had* been out a lot, overseeing the work at Chick-O-Rama and traveling back and forth to Bridgeport to get her new college courses settled. Someone honked and yelled at her and she waved, then turned back to Ryan. "You said you needed to tell me something."

"I do, but not here."

"Here's where I am," she said shortly. "If you want to talk with me so badly, you better start soon." She turned and walked away. She knew she was being rude, knew she was even being obstinate, but she didn't know how else to act. She felt angry and betrayed and a week away from him hadn't lessened her feelings.

"I'm not going to walk up and down this road next to a woman dressed up like a chicken," Ryan said from somewhere behind her, "and pour out how much I love her, when all I can see is her legs."

She came to an abrupt halt. "What did you say?"

"I said I love you."

She stopped walking. "Well, you've got a fine way of proving it," she said, her voice trembling. "You go to my uncle behind my back and give him a loan and—"

"And what?"

She turned around. "And didn't *tell* me," she said, her voice wavering with emotion. "That's why I'm so mad, Ryan—your not telling me, and telling Henry not to tell me. How could I help but be suspicious of you?" She was suddenly angry at the chicken head that kept her from seeing Ryan more clearly. They had enough obstacles between them; they didn't need another. She reached up and whipped off the bulky headpiece, and her black hair swirled rebelliously around her head in the breeze. "Can you understand that?" she asked, her voice low and vibrating with anger. "Can you see what it looked like to me, on top of all the other stuff I'd just read in the paper?"

"What did you expect me to do?" he asked, sounding as angry as she. "Call you in to sit around a conference table and suggest I float a loan for you? Do you think you'd have listened if I had?"

"I'd have listened."

He shook his head. "No, you wouldn't have. You were too busy seeing spooks under every bed. I couldn't do anything even remotely related to this business without making you think I wanted to take it over."

She searched his eyes. "What *do* you want, Ryan?"

"I want you," he said, sounding grim. "I want you and I don't know how to tell you how much I want you. I want you and I'm scared to death that you won't want me." He ran a hand through his hair. "I know I screwed up, Cass. I went behind your back. I see that now, but..." He shook his head and ran a hand over the nape of his neck as he stared at the ground. "Cass, there's only one thing I'm good at—running a business." He raised his head and met her eyes, and his voice lowered, losing some of its intensity. "I've never been very good at anything else." He reached out and fingered a strand of her hair. "Remember once I told you we were a lot alike?"

She nodded, and he went on, "You told me you're afraid to trust men. Hell, I'm afraid to trust anyone, not just women. Business is cutthroat, so I've felt at home in it. But relationships, they require trust, and I..." He shook his head, looking tired. "I've never been big on that, Cass. I've come a long way, and I thought I'd learned all the lessons I needed to learn, then I met you and the first thing I did was whip out my checkbook and offer to buy you out. That's the only way I know how to relate to people, Cass—by challenging them. I never wanted Chick-O-Rama—I couldn't care less about it. From the start I wanted you, but I didn't know how to approach you, so I made a game out of it, to test you, to see if you had as much spirit as you seemed to have."

"Do I?" she asked, her voice softer, her eyes filled with something very close to sadness.

"More than me," he said, eyes locked on hers. "You at least were honest enough to tell me about Geoff and how he hurt you. I've kept almost everything about myself from you."

"You could still tell me," she said. "I mean, it's not as if we only had three weeks together to get to know each other.

You'll be busy, of course, and so will I when I go back to school, but—"

"School?" He searched her eyes, a smile growing on his face. "You're going back to school?"

She nodded, beginning to smile. "You gave me some good advice, St. James. I decided to stop being a fool and take it."

"I'm glad, Cass. You're too intelligent to sentence yourself to drudge jobs all your life." He looked at the sparkling facade of the new Chick-O-Rama. "And once you and Henry get your feet on the ground, you'll be able to get a loan from the bank to pay mine back—you'll be on your way. And with a degree, you'll have the knowledge to grow." He looked back at her and smiled. "Hell, maybe someday Chick-O-Rama will grow as big as Burger City."

She didn't say anything. Right now, Chick-O-Rama didn't concern her. What Ryan had to say did. But he had to want to tell her, whatever it was. She wasn't going to force him. "So," she said, pulling the headpiece back over her head. "I'm afraid I have to work, Ryan. Maybe I'll see you around sometime."

He stared at her, looking as if he wasn't going to let her end the conversation, then he finally nodded. "Okay, Cass, see you around." Turning, he walked back to his motorcycle, his head down, his shoulders slumped.

She stood and watched him walk away, her heart dipping. She'd thought he'd convince her to leave work early. Instead, he looked as if he were walking out of her life. She raised a hand and almost called out to him, then she lowered it as he kicked his cycle to life and roared off. Turning, she stared at the new facade of Chick-O-Rama, and for the first time, wondered if it could possibly replace Ryan St. James.

* * *

"But, Uncle Henry, I don't want to wear the chicken outfit again," Cass said irritably. "It's hot and it weighs a ton. It was a cute gimmick, but its time is past." A week had gone by, but Ryan hadn't called. Cass didn't want to wear the damned chicken outfit again, if only because it reminded her so vividly of Ryan. Every time she wore it, he seemed to magically appear.

"Ha," said Henry. "Just wear it for me this one last time, hunh?"

"Why?" she asked. "You're not even working tomorrow. One of the new teenagers you hired will be in, so you won't even be around to see me."

"Just humor an old man, will you? Just once, huh? I want to come by and take a snapshot of you out front."

Cass lifted wide eyes. "Why, Henry," she said gently, "you old softie. Why didn't you tell me that's what you wanted me to wear it for?"

Henry ran a finger around the rim of his shirt collar as if he were uncomfortable. "Agh, Cassie," he said, unable to meet her eyes.

"All right, Henry," she said, smiling at his embarrassment at being found out. "I'll wear it this one last time, just for you."

He raised his head and beamed at her, and she frowned and narrowed her eyes. There was something about that smile of his, something fishy.... "Are you up to something, Henry?" she asked.

"Me?" He rested a beefy hand on his heart. "Up to something? What would I be up to?" He leaned forward and kissed her on the cheek. "I just wanna get a picture of my only niece, that's all."

Reassured, Cass smiled warmly. "Okay, Henry. Tomorrow, promptly at noon, I'll be outside with my silly costume on."

"Good," Henry said, his blue eyes sparkling merrily.
"Perfect."

The next morning, when Cass went to look for her Sunday paper, it was missing. She shrugged it off and made a note to deduct the price from the paperboy's next payment, then ate breakfast quickly and drove to work, where the chicken outfit awaited her.

As she approached Chick-O-Rama, she glanced at Burger City and noticed a crowd milling around. Frowning, she wondered what was going on. Maybe Henry had been smart—maybe it was a good idea for her to wear the chicken outfit. She'd be outside, trying to draw the crowds away from Burger City.

She struggled into her chicken outfit, then took up her hand-lettered sign and made her way outside. It was another beautiful late summer day, with a clear blue sky and the promise of fall in the air. Up the street, one maple tree had already started to turn scarlet. A single limb stuck out over the street, its leaves blazing against the vivid blue of the sky.

Cass hoisted her sign and walked toward the street, her eyes drawn to the crowd at Burger City. She frowned and gestured at a policeman sitting in his car at the curb. "What's going on over at Burger City today?" she asked.

"Didn't you read the paper this morning?" he asked, chuckling. "They had a big ad in it. You got yourself some competition, Charlie."

"Competition?" She turned and looked across the street, then heard the Dixieland band strike up "As The Saints Go Marching In." At the same moment, a gigantic banner was unfurled over the roof of Burger City. Cass started at it, openmouthed.

BURGER CITY, it read, HOME OF CHUCK THE CONTENTED COW.

"Chuck, the contented—" She bit off the last of the words and stalked toward the sidewalk, her legs flashing in their gilt-spangled panty hose. Just as she reached the sidewalk, a giant roar went up and she spied Chuck. She came to a stop and simply stared, astounded.

It wasn't a cow, of course. It was obviously two men in a cow costume, prancing and dancing around, bowing to the crowd and mooing, causing the kids in the crowd at Burger City to howl with delight. Cass put her hands in their chicken-web gloves on her inflated, feather-covered hips and glared at the cow. How dare they steal her idea.

No one was paying even the remotest attention to her, she realized. She could stand out here all day but the fascination with the damned cow would keep everyone from even looking at her. She took a deep breath and tried to calm her racing heart. She was sure her blood pressure was sky-high and—

She broke off, horrified. It was coming this way, making a beeline—if the gangling thing were capable of making such a thing as a beeline—straight for her. The crowd was laughing, and the cow was pointing at her and waving its own sign that said something about trying the burgers at Burger City.

That was all she needed. Standing there, feathers quivering with agitation, she waited for the cow to cross the street. That cow was coming onto chicken territory!

"I suppose you think this is funny," she said when the cow reached her side of the street.

"Yup," said a low voice.

She cocked her chicken head and narrowed her eyes, wondering who it was under that ridiculous getup. The cow's head was as silly as her chicken head, with plastic horns, pointy ears, and large brown eyes that barely revealed the man's eyes beneath. Briefly, she wondered if whoever it was in there had gotten the costume from the same costumer.

"You're on private property on this side of the street," she said coolly. "Please refrain from putting a hoof on my parking lot."

Purposely disobeying, the cow put a foot out and stepped on the parking lot. Cass stared, astounded. "Who are you?" she demanded. "I'll have you fired! I know the owner of Burger City, you know!"

A familiar-sounding snicker emanated from the rear of the cow, causing Cass to do a double take. She knew that laugh! Frowning, she tried to remember where she'd heard it.

The back part of the cow punched the front part and hissed at it, then the front part hissed back. Cass's eyes narrowed even further. She took a step closer. "Who are you?" she asked suspiciously.

"A friend."

She stared, incredulous. *"Ryan?"*

"Yup," said the voice.

"Why you..." She quivered and realized that some of her feathers were coming off her costume and floating in the air around her. "*What* do you think you're *doing*?" she said under her breath, backing away as the crowd began to assemble around them.

There was no response, then the back part of the cow poked the front part, which she now knew was Ryan. "Go on," the familiar voice said, "tell her, for cryin' out loud."

"Uncle *Henry*?" She stared at the back end, astounded, then almost keeled over when she heard him say, "Yes, it's Uncle Henry. Now I know why you don't like wearing that costume, Cass. It's *hot* in here!"

"And it's going to get hotter," she said from between gritted teeth.

"She sounds mad. Talk to her, Ryan, before she does something she'll regret."

Ryan reached up and took the cow head off, then began to unzip the costume. Cass just stared openmouthed as the crowd went wild, laughing and pointing. Ryan stepped out of the costume, and Henry's head peered from the opening. Cass didn't know what to do, so she just kept standing there.

"It wasn't Henry's idea," Ryan said, trying to fight a grin. "I made him do it."

"But he went along with it," she said, trying to infuse some ice into her words. But it just wasn't working. She had the strangest desire to laugh, and it was getting harder and harder to keep from doing it.

"Yeah, well, it seemed a good idea at the time," Ryan said, and then he did grin.

"And now?" she asked, still trying to fight the smile that threatened to overwhelm her.

"Now," Ryan said, "I think I've got a better idea." He gestured toward the street and a long, silver limousine appeared miraculously as if from thin air.

Ryan swept Cass into his arms. Whooping with surprise, she flung her arms around him, clinging to him for dear life. "What are you *doing*?" she cried, beginning to laugh.

"Kidnapping you," Ryan said, laughing with her. "Or chicknapping, I guess."

"Put me down," she said, not very effectively. She was laughing harder now, and clinging to him with all her strength.

The chauffeur got out and opened the door, and Ryan deposited her in the seat next to the driver, then ran around the car and got into the driver's seat. "I hope you don't mind, Cass," he said, waving goodbye to the chauffeur and driving off. "But I wanted to get your attention today."

Cass dragged off the heavy chicken head. "Don't you think this was a little drastic?"

Ryan's grin disappeared. "No," he said, suddenly serious. "I think I'd do anything to convince you how much I love you."

Cass felt strange shivers cascade over her, then she leaned over and kissed him on the cheek. "You're a strange man, Ryan St. James," she murmured. "But I love you, too."

The candles cast a warm glow on the dining room table, a Mozart concerto played softly in the background, and ghostly moonlight lay on the meadows outside, bathing the world in silver light. Cass sat with her chin resting on her folded hands, her elbows propped on the shining surface of the table. Across from her, Ryan talked of his decision to stop marketing Chicken Chunx.

"You were right, Cass," he said. "They were just so-so. Burger Kingdom's Chicken Nibbles are ten times better. I've decided to stick to what I know best—burgers and fries."

"That's probably for the best," she said quietly. She stood up and went to the sliding glass doors overlooking the deck. A weather front had swept into Connecticut, cooling the August night so that it felt like mid-September. Cass rubbed her arms. She'd worn only a sleeveless white blouse and shorts under her chicken costume. Now she wished she had a sweater. Ryan came up behind her and put his hands on her upper arms and began to rub them softly.

"Cool?" he asked, his voice low and gentle.

She nodded, then smiled when he wrapped his arms around her and drew her back against him. He nuzzled the soft skin of her neck beneath her ear.

She turned to face him, seeing anxiety and tension etched in the lines around his mouth and between his eyes. Reaching up, she smoothed her hand over his cheek. "You look so tired, Ryan, and so worried."

Taking a deep breath, he took her by the hand and led her into the living room. "I need to talk to you, Cass, to explain some things about myself."

She stroked his cheek, then leaned over and kissed him gently. "Okay," she murmured. "Tell me. What's the horrible secret you're afraid to share?"

A muscle jumped in his cheek as he looked directly into her eyes. "Remember that day we drove to Salisbury and you asked what made me tick? We were talking about my childhood, and I mentioned that some things had filled me with this hunger to succeed, as if by becoming successful, I could show everyone who'd hurt me and called me names that I was better than they were."

She took his hand and held it. "I guess a lot of us think that way, Ryan," she said softly. "That sounds pretty normal to me."

Ryan nodded, looking down, his face in shadows. "There was one name they called me a lot, Cass." She didn't say anything, just held his hand, waiting. He raised his head and looked at her. "They used to call me bastard, but it didn't bother me until I found out why."

She frowned slightly. "What do you mean?"

"I've told you about my mother," he said. "But I haven't mentioned my father."

"No," she said, beginning to suspect what was to come. "You haven't."

"He died two weeks before he and my mother were going to be married, Cass," he said, looking directly into her eyes.

As the words slowly sank in, things began to make sense to Cass. She pictured Ryan, young and fatherless, enduring taunts and ridicule, and she felt the pain he must have felt rise up inside her, aching in its intensity. She squeezed his hand, but waited, knowing he had more to say. He had to share it all, in his own way and his own time, before he could totally trust her acceptance and love.

"So you see, Cass," he continued, "I was literally a bastard. My mother never married, so I still am for that matter. We lived in this small hick town where everyone looked at her as if she wore the scarlet letter. When I was real young, I didn't understand. I guess I was about ten or eleven when I overheard some people talking and it finally sank in that my mother hadn't been married when I was born."

Cass felt her heart constrict with pain for him. "Ryan," she said softly, "that doesn't matter. The way you were born doesn't count."

"It mattered in that town," he said grimly. "And it mattered to the woman I was engaged to. She was from a small town herself, brought up to care about what people thought. She wanted everything to *look* right, wanted everything perfect in life. When I told her what had happened to my mother and father, she was shocked. She couldn't understand that they'd been trapped by a cruel twist of fate. They'd been engaged for two years when they couldn't stop themselves one night. It was a couple months before their wedding day and my mom got pregnant." His eyes grew warm in memory and he smiled tenderly. "She told me they both were so happy." His smile faded. "Then one night, two weeks before their wedding day, my father was driving her to her house, when a drunk driver plowed into his car."

She put her arms around him and held him. "Oh, Ryan," she breathed. "How horrible for your mom."

Ryan rubbed her arms, his eyes focused on the past. "That's what made Ryan St. James run, Cass. All those years of being the town outcast, being laughed at and pointed at and scorned. When I was old enough, I quit school and joined the army. At the time, it seemed the only path open to me. I just wanted to run away, get as far away from her and that town as I could."

"Get away from your mother?"

He nodded. "When I was young, before I went into the army, I blamed her for what happened. She'd raised me so damned strict, always telling me how wrong it was to try to sleep with a girl before you married, and then I found out she had done just that. I called her a hypocrite, and gave her a pretty hard time. I began to grow up in the army though, and it finally sank into this thick skull of mine that I loved her. I finally understood that what happened to her and my father wasn't anyone's fault. It was just..." He lifted his shoulders. "It was just life, Cass," he said. "Just life..."

She hugged him silently, unable to speak.

"You have to understand, Cass. I don't want to bring a child into the world if there's any possibility that the same thing could happen to him. I feel such an obligation to be responsible, not to get carried away by physical feelings that could have such a detrimental effect on someone's life." He brushed her hair back from her forehead, his eyes lovingly exploring her face. "I love you so much, Cass, that I can finally understand what happened to my parents, because they were so much in love. But I realized it could happen to me, too, and to you, and to our child, and so I used all the strength I have to resist giving in to wanting you so badly."

"Oh, Ryan," she said, finally understanding. She searched his face. "I thought it meant you didn't want to get trapped into marrying anyone, you were afraid I'd tie you down, like Geoff. Why didn't you tell me?"

"I couldn't tell you," he said. "I was a coward. All these years, it seemed like the blackest blot on my character, as if I walked around with a scarlet *B* plastered on me."

She just held him tightly, realizing at last how harmful their suppositions had been. Instead of talking, they'd both jumped to conclusions. "Oh, Ryan," she said, "we've been such fools."

He frowned thoughtfully. "I don't know about that, Cass. Maybe people have to work out their fears before they

can learn to trust someone. Maybe it would be more foolish to go into a relationship with blind trust. Maybe what
we've gone through is exactly what we needed to find out
how much we care about each other." He looked into her
eyes and his frown changed magically into a smile. "Maybe
this was the only way we could have a future together,
Cass."

"Do we have a future?" she asked softly, her eyes filled
with quiet joy.

"We have a future," he said. "The question is, can a
successful burger man marry a successful chicken lady
without ruffling her feathers? And if they do marry, will
they have time for two or three kids and a home life? The
burger man is tired of life in the fast lane, and he wants to
settle down. But the chicken lady is just starting out, and
maybe she'll want to spread her wings and fly a little, and if
that's the case, maybe she won't marry the burger guy. And
if that's the case—"

She put a finger against his lips. "Be quiet," she whispered. "She'll marry him."

"You'll marry me?" he asked, breaking into a grin.

She nodded, smiling. "You're right about my wanting to
spread my wings and fly a little, but why can't we fly together? I love you, Ryan," she said softly. "No matter how
successful I eventually become, it wouldn't be as sweet if I
weren't sharing it with you."

He brushed his fingertips over her cheek, his eyes filled
with love. "All my life, I've wanted to be loved, accepted for
myself, and now I've found that with you. I feel so lucky,
Cass, and so happy."

She nodded, her eyes beginning to fill with mist. "I
know," she said, her throat tight with emotion. She hugged
him and felt the heat of his arms around her, wrapping her
in love. "It's what I've wanted, too, Ryan, and what I
wouldn't let myself dare to hope for." She lifted her head to

gaze into his eyes. "Let's try to make it work," she whispered.

"It will," he said. "We'll work at it together, one step at a time...."

Then he smiled, and in his eyes, she saw the future.

*   *   *   *   *